The GIRL, the CAT & the NAVIGATOR

Matilda Woods
Illustrated by Anuska Allepuz

SCHOLASTIC

Scholastic Children's Books
An imprint of Scholastic Ltd
Euston House, 24 Eversholt Street, London, NW1 1DB, UK
Registered office: Westfield Road, Southam, Warwickshire, CV47 0RA
SCHOLASTIC and associated logos are trademarks and/or
registered trademarks of Scholastic Inc.

First published in the UK by Scholastic Ltd, 2018

Text copyright © Matilda Woods, 2018
Illustration copyright © Anuska Allepuz, 2018

The right of Matilda Woods and Anuska Allepuz to be identified
as the author and illustrator of this work has been asserted.

ISBN 978 1407 18490 6

Printed by CPI Group (UK) Ltd, Croydon, CR0 4YY
Papers used by Scholastic Children's Books are made
from wood grown in sustainable forests.

1 3 5 7 9 10 8 6 4 2

www.scholastic.co.uk

For Boots and Sally and Alice and Gandolf
Four very adventurous cats

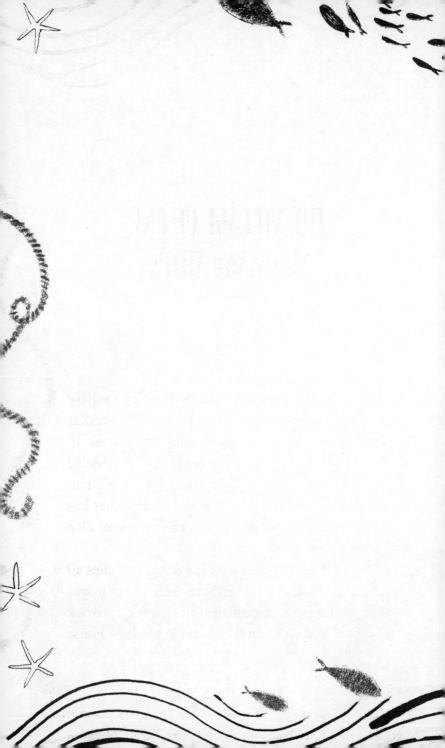

THE VILLAGE OF ONE
THOUSAND SHIPS

In the wild and white North, there is a village that has two names. The first name is Nordlor and comes from the man who discovered it: Fredrick Nordlor, the great explorer who sailed further into the Northern Sea than any man before. And the second name – the name that has made it famous worldwide – is the Village of One Thousand Ships.

Nordlor sits beside a long fjord that stretches all the way to the Great Northern Sea. When it was first settled no trees grew nearby, so when Fredrick Nordlor wanted to build the village's first house he did not have many options. He built one with snow, but it melted when the spring thaw came. He weaved a house from grass, but it turned brittle and crumbled in the summer. He even built a home from seashells dredged out of the fjord, but when winter came there were so many gaps in the walls that it felt colder inside than out.

In desperation, Fredrick Nordlor pulled apart his own ship and used the wood to build a house. It worked a lot better than the snow and the grass and the shells he had used before. But there was one peculiarity. Even in summer the house was cold and wet, and every night it rocked back and forth like the ship still sailed upon the sea instead of standing broken on land.

Fredrick Nordlor thought this peculiarity was limited to the wood pulled from his own ship, but when another boat washed aground and was used to build the village hall, the same thing happened. It was like the wood from northern ships possessed a special power that made it hold on to the memories it made while still at sea.

Fredrick Nordlor liked this trait in the wood – "It gives it a sense of northern character," he would say – and so, even when trees were planted in the mountains around the village, it became tradition

Libraries NI

Your Library Doesn't End Here
Get free eBooks and eMagazines
ariesni.org.uk/pages/lniebooksandemagazi
Or ask Staff for details
Moira Library
21a Backwood Road
Moira
BT67 0LJ
Tel 028 9261 9330

Borrowed Items 08/02/2020 10:33
XXXXXX6533

Item Title	Due Date
The girl, the cat the navigator	29/02/2020

Thank you for visiting Moira Library.

Email: moira.library@librariesni.org.uk
www.librariesni.org.uk

Moira Library
21a Backwood Road
Moira
BT67 0LJ
Tel 028 9261 9330

Borrowed Items 08/02/2020 10:32

XXXXXXX1352

Item Title	Due Date
Erebus : the story of a ship	29/02/2020
Real food kids will love : over	29/02/2020
100 simple and delicious recipes for toddlers and up	
Down to earth : gardening wisdom from Monty	29/02/2020

Thank you for visiting Moira Library.

for all the buildings in Nordlor to be made from sunken ships.

Over the years, whenever a whaler sank, or even just a small fishing boat, it was dredged into Nordlor Harbour, pulled apart and built back up into something new. And that is how the village of Nordlor grew. Houses went up, a dock was built and taverns lined the shore.

As Nordlor itself grew, so too did its reputation. Soon, people all over the North and South spoke about the village built from sunken ships.

"Fredrick Nordlor had the idea himself," a man from Islo said. "He always was a smart one."

"I heard he got the idea from his wife," whispered a woman in Iceblown Harbour. "Behind every great man is an even greater woman telling him what to do."

"Apparently," swore a boy in Whitlock, "the village is made from exactly one thousand sunken ships and not a single one more."

Nordlor became so famous that a prince in the South spent two thousand golden crowns to have a replica built within the walls of his castle. Little Nordlor, it was called, and he refused to let any member of the public see it.

But for a village where everyone wanted to go,

3

hardly anyone actually ever went there. The snow was too deep, the air was too cold and the days were too short and dark.

It was so rare for people to come to Nordlor that when a new person arrived it always caused a stir. Like the time Lady Summer left the South and took up residence in Whalebone Lane. Or the time Mister Bjorkman fled Mournful Harbour and built a tower out of ship masts in the main square. But the one visitor who caused the greatest stir of all was the fortune teller, Freydis Spits.

THE FORTUNE TELLER'S
FIRST PREDICTION

The fortune teller arrived in the middle of a deep winter night. She travelled by carriage: one of the grandest carriages the North had ever seen. It was encrusted with jewels, engraved with golden whales and, instead of being led by the traditional two horses, this carriage was led by four polar bears. To stop the bears from biting her, the fortune teller had locked them in golden chains and each wore a golden muzzle around its snout.

The polar bears lumbered along the sea cobbles that lined the village, the chains that weighed them

down clinking in the night. Despite looking grand, the bears were cumbersome and slow. The fortune teller pulled them to a stop beneath a green-and-silver sign that read: *The Sinking Eel*.

The Sinking Eel was the most popular tavern in Nordlor. Before it was dredged out of the sea and hauled into the village it had been a grand ship called the *Slippery Eel*. But then it hit an iceberg and sank sixty miles north of Fisherman's Hell. Yet despite this happening fifty years before, it appeared to still be in the throes of sinking. Icy ocean water dripped from the roof, waves smashed against the bar and, if it was very windy, you could just make out the screams of men as they scurried to stay above the rising water.

"That's me," old man Eirik would say to anybody who would listen. "That's me. The one screaming, 'Oh, Lords and Ladies of the Sea. We're going down!'"

The fortune teller climbed off her carriage and knocked on the tavern door. When no one answered, she scowled and opened it herself.

"Behold!" the fortune teller cried as she stepped into the tavern. The weather in the North was wild that night and rain, hail and sleet followed her inside. "It is I, Freydis Spits: the famed fortune

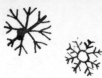

teller of the North!" She threw her arms out wide and fifty seashells that hung from a golden staff over her shoulder rattled in applause. "There's no reading tea leaves in a cup for me," she said to the village folk who had gathered for a relaxing evening drink and were now glaring at her, annoyed at the interruption. "No. No. That type of fortune telling won't do. And don't you dare speak to me of lines on a palm. There's no future in that. I only search for the future in one place: in the shells that wash ashore from the Great Northern Sea."

A curious hush fell over the gathered crowd. It was a well-known fact that the shells which washed ashore from the Great Northern Sea didn't just capture the sounds of the ocean: of waves and seals and whales singing deep into the night. They also held whisperings – little tinklings – of things that had yet to come. Very few people could hear what these whisperings were. So those that could were held in high esteem.

"These shells upon my back," Freydis said, "have all whispered great secrets to me. This green one here" – she untied a piece of rope that held one of the shells to her golden staff – "foretold the sinking of the *Great Red Fish* twenty years before it was even built. And this one here" – she untied a shell that glinted faintly orange – "knew about the Great Fire of Mournful Harbour three nights before the spark was lit. And this one" – she pointed to a third shell – "told me that the great whaler *Roe* would sink to the bottom of the Icelands on its maiden voyage."

The curious hush that had fallen over the tavern when the fortune teller first arrived was broken by laughter.

"The *Roe* didn't sink, you fool!" one of the men yelled. "She docked in this very village not two weeks past."

"Exactly," Freydis said. "I sold them that fortune, didn't I? So, they changed their course and thirty men survived. It would have sunk if they hadn't listened to me. And now," Freydis said before anyone else could interrupt, "I have heard a whispering about a person in this very village: in the village of Nordlor."

The men in the tavern looked at one another. They wondered who the fortune was for. Before they could guess, Freydis pulled a purple shell from the depths of her elk-skin cloak and held it up for them to see.

"Here, within this shell," she said, "are whispers of something that has yet to come. Something that

9

will change the life of a man called Captain Britt."

All eyes turned to one man sitting alone at the back of the tavern.

"You have a future for me?" the man said softly. Even though he was seated, he towered above those around him. He had a black beard and a face weathered by the wind and spray of the Northern Sea.

"If you are Captain Britt, then, aye, it is for you," Freydis replied.

"What is it?" the man said. "What does it say?"

Freydis cackled with delight. "A fortune teller has to make her own fortune somehow. I'm not going to tell you the fortune, not until you pay for it."

"How much?" the man said.

Freydis thought about this for some time. Normally she charged two silvers for a fortune of this kind. But she knew the man before her was very wealthy; after all, he was the captain and owner of the largest whaling ship in Nordlor. So, she decided to charge him more. "It will cost you a golden crown."

This time it was Captain Britt who laughed. "Not a chance," he said and turned back to his drink.

"Are you sure?" Freydis asked. She moved closer. "I'm certain it is a future you would very much like to hear."

Perhaps because he was a gambling man, or perhaps because he feared his ship might be the next one to sink, Captain Britt reconsidered her offer.

"Five silvers," he said. "And not a copper more."

"Done!" Freydis snatched the offered coins and buried them deep in the folds of her cloak. Then, she raised the purple shell to her ear and listened once more to the future inside. When she had the words just right, she repeated them for all the men in the tavern to hear:

AFTER THE BIRTH OF SIX DISAPPOINTING DAUGHTERS, CAPTAIN BRITT OF THE *PLUCKY LEOPARD* WILL FINALLY BECOME THE PROUD FATHER OF A BOLD AND BRAVE SON.

A PARTY AT THE SINKING EEL

Nine Months Later

"Drinks on me!" Captain Britt yelled as more and more people streamed into the Sinking Eel. Nine months had passed since he purchased the fortune teller's prediction, and now he had invited the whole village to celebrate the birth of his son.

"No. You haven't missed it," he said as another person entered the tavern. He wondered if he should have chosen a different setting for the celebration. It might be bad luck to have it inside a sinking ship. But it was too late now. His son was almost here.

"Come on, woman," the captain growled under his breath. "Get a move on." The bill at the bar was growing by the minute. Perhaps it had been a mistake to invite the whole village. At least he hadn't opened any of the expensive bottles of wine. He was saving them for when his son arrived: he was going to cut them open with his whalebone knife and spray the whole crowd.

The captain's wife wailed and screamed for another two hours. Her cries were so loud they carried all the way from her home to the inn. The beer flowed. The crowd grew. The music played. The barman even gave a few nips of spirits to the children, and now the captain's daughters were stumbling about like six bowling pins about to topple down. Then, a new cry rattled the tavern windows. It was the cry of the birthing lady.

All sounds of celebration stopped. Silence fell upon the inn. It was broken five minutes later when a very nervous looking woman entered the room. She held a small bundle in her arms.

"What is it?" the captain said, hurrying towards her. "What's wrong? Has something happened to my son? Oh, Lords and Ladies of the Sea," he wailed. "He isn't dead, is he?"

The birthing lady shook her head. "No. It's not that Captain. It's just..."

"Yes?" The captain stepped closer. "Go on. What are you waiting for, woman? Tell me the good news."

"Well, um..." The birthing lady stared at the floor. "Your wife has given birth to a girl."

"Girl?" The captain's face fell. "No." He shook his head. "That can't be right. I've already got six of them. Check again."

Though she doubted anything had changed, the birthing lady glanced down at the child in her arms. "I'm sorry," she said. "I can assure you, Captain, it is a girl. A beautiful, healthy baby girl."

"But..." The captain looked from the child to the woman holding it. "I'm meant to have a son. I only want a son." He reached for his whalebone knife. "Where is she?" he growled. "Where is that bloody fortune teller?"

A nervous hush fell over the gathered crowd. Everywhere heads turned, searching for a woman dressed in elk skin and clutching a staff full of shells. But out of everyone who lived in the village, the fortune teller was one of only a handful who weren't there.

"Get out of my way," the captain growled as he pushed a path towards the door. "I'm going to

14

wring her neck!" he cried. "I'm going to gut her like a dead fish. I'm going to cut her up like whale blubber. She's dead, you hear me? The woman is dead!"

And with that, the captain left his new daughter and stormed off into the night.

Two lanes away from the Sinking Eel, in a small cottage hewn from the bow of a boat called the *Little Skipper*, another child was being born.

"You're doing splendidly, Mathilde," a man said to his wife. "Absolutely splendid." The man was smoking an old pipe engraved with whales and fish, but it kept falling out of his mouth. He was nervous. He had never helped deliver a child before. But the town's only birthing lady was at the captain's house, so it was all up to him. "You're almost there," he said to his wife with a warm smile.

The man's wife smiled back. They had wanted a child for over twenty years, and now their dream was coming true. Unlike Captain Britt, they did not care if it was a boy or a girl, only that it was healthy and happy and loved by the two of them.

Two more hours passed. Mathilde grew tired and weak, but with her husband's encouragement she kept on trying. Finally, after a third hour went by, she gave birth. A silence fell upon the home.

"Haroyld," she said. "Is it a he or a she?"

"A she," Haroyld said sadly.

Mathilde laughed. "You said you didn't mind which it was. But I knew you wanted a son. Men always want sons."

"It's not that," Haroyld said. "It's. . ." Slowly, he held the baby up. She was not moving.

"Oh, Haroyld." Mathilde gasped. "Please no."

"I am so sorry, Mathilde." Haroyld wrapped the baby in a yellow blanket and walked over to his wife.

"She's beautiful," Mathilde said.

"As beautiful as the Northern Lights," Haroyld agreed. He stroked the baby's cold cheek with his thumb and rocked her gently. Even though she was already gone, he did not want to let his only daughter go.

THE CAPTAIN'S SEVENTH DAUGHTER

Ten Years Later

"Ah-ha!" Oona Britt said. "Here it is. My whalebone knife." She leant down and picked a large stick off the ground. Every great captain in the North owned a whalebone knife. That's what her father said. He wore his knife tied with a rope around his waist, and only ever took it off when he was about to make a kill.

"Now, where has my ship gone?" Oona looked up and down the harbour. She could just make out the silhouette of the *Plucky Leopard* bobbing in the water. The ship belonged to her father, but today

she would pretend it was hers. "Come on, Gillbert," she said to a toy cat balancing on her shoulder. "Time to get on board. We'll be late for the Great Hunt."

Oona did not move closer to the ship. Instead, she pretended to board it from where she stood. She climbed an invisible plank and looked out across the water. She imagined she was just like her father when he went on the Great Hunt.

During the Great Hunt one ship from every northern village set sail for the Icelands: a place so cold that if you stayed there long enough the sea would freeze around you and you could walk to the top of the world. Each crew would hunt for a whale. If they caught one, they'd cut it up and bring it back to the village where it was used to make all sorts of things. Meat and blubber were used for food: in winter one bowl of blubber soup could keep a man full for a whole week. Whale oil and whale wax were used for lamps and candles that burned safely and brightly all through the night. And whalebones were shipped south and used to make corsets and parasols for all the southern ladies.

The Great Hunt was very dangerous; one in ten ships sunk during each hunt and only half were lucky enough to catch a whale. But despite the dire odds, Oona's father had caught a whale every single year. It was a record that had never been broken.

"Ahoy, Gillbert," Oona cried to her knitted cat. In the North, every ship had a cat. No one really knew for sure where they came from. But at some point between the plans being drawn up and the rudder being put in, a cat would inevitably appear on the deck. For as long as the ship sailed the cat would sail with it.

Oona had heard there was a saying in the South: a saying that the captain goes down with their ship. But up here in the North it was the cat who sank into the sea and the captain who was the first into the whaleboat.

"Ahoy," Oona cried again. "A whale. I see a whale. We must take chase. But be quiet," she warned the toy cat. "We do not want to gally the beast." Oona crouched down and crawled along the black sand that lined Nordlor's shore. She was about to catch the imagined beast, when someone stood on the end of her stick and snapped it in two.

"Oops," came a voice, but it did not sound at all sorry.

Oona's mind reluctantly left the Icelands and returned to the village of Nordlor. She looked up and her heart sank. In front of her stood her six sisters: Ina, Berit, Sissel, Trine and the twins, Onka and Plonka.

Oona dropped her broken stick and stood up.

"What are you doing here?" Her sisters never came down to the shore. That was precisely why she spent so much time there.

"We've come to fetch you," Ina said. "Mother and Father are taking us to lunch."

"And I'm allowed to come?" Oona said. She couldn't believe it. Usually when her family went out for lunch they made her stay at home alone.

"Apparently, they want to tell us something, and it's important we're all there to hear."

Oona dusted the black sand off her clothes. She was almost ready to go when one of her sisters spotted the toy cat sticking out of her pocket.

"What is that?" Berit said with a scowl.

"It's a sea cat," Oona replied. "He's called Gillbert."

"It looks like a plain old land cat to me."

"No it isn't. Can't you see his eyes? They're blue and have waves in them."

"Where did you even get it?" Sissel asked.

"I bet she got it out of a bin," Onka said. "A great, big, dirty bin."

"Or maybe she made it herself," Plonka said

with a snigger. "That would explain the poor workmanship."

"Gillbert isn't poorly made," Oona said. "He's perfect."

"Really?" Berit asked. "Let me see." Before Oona could step away, Berit grabbed Gillbert and yanked him from her arms. Then, she ripped off one of his ears.

"Stop it," Oona said. She tried to grab her cat, but Onka and Plonka held her back. "You're breaking him."

"If he wasn't so poorly made, he wouldn't be so easy to break." To demonstrate this, Berit ripped off Gillbert's tail and then used her teeth to pull out his eyes. She spat them on the ground and stomped them into the sand. "There," she said. "He looks a lot better now."

"You lardy catfish!" Oona yelled. "You slimy eel!" She broke free of Onka and Plonka and picked up a rock. She threw it at Berit's head. "Give him back! Give him back now, or I'll – I'll. . ."

"Or you'll what?" Berit said. "You'll tell Mother and Father?"

All of Oona's sisters laughed except for the youngest, Trine. Trine looked like she wanted her sisters to stop teasing Oona. But she was too frightened to speak up.

"They don't care about you," Berit continued. "They never have and they never will. You were meant to be a boy. Not another stupid girl."

"That's not true," Oona cried. "You're all just a bunch of – a bunch of lying, wobbly walruses!"

That hit her sisters deep. They all knew they looked like walruses, what with their greyish complexion and protruding teeth. Oona was the only one to avoid the misfortune of resembling one of them. She was small and delicate, like the first wild flowers that bloomed in spring.

"How dare you," Berit said. "Mother told you you're not allowed to call us that."

"Yeah," Oona's other five sisters added. "Not ever!"

"Well, I did. And I'm not taking it back. Not until you give me Gillbert."

"All right," Berit said. "You can have Gillbert." She pulled back her arm and threw the toy cat into the harbour. "There you go," she said with a smirk. "He's all yours."

"You're late," Oona's father said when she met her family outside the Rusted Anchor. It was one of five taverns in Nordlor. There used to be six, but on the day of Oona's birth, the Sinking Eel had mysteriously burned to the ground. Many suspected Oona's father of the crime, such had been his rage that night. But no evidence had been found, and so the crime remained unsolved.

"I'm sorry," Oona said. She had spent thirty minutes trying to fish Gillbert out of the water. But her rescue mission had failed, and the knitted cat now lay forever lost at the bottom of Nordlor Harbour.

"Typical," her father mumbled. He turned and entered the tavern.

"It used to be called the Golden Anchor," Oona told her sisters as they followed their father inside. "But then it sank in a storm. One soul was lost and twenty others were saved."

"We don't care," Oona's five oldest sisters said at once. Trine was about to say something different, but before she could her older sisters grabbed her and barged into the tavern. One of the only times they moved quickly was when there was the promise of food ahead.

Oona sighed and followed her sisters inside. She knew a lot about ships; at least, she knew about the ones that had sunk. She owned a book all about them. But her father's ship was a different story. Despite being the sole owner and captain of the *Plucky Leopard*, he had never let one of his daughters on board. Oona's sisters did not mind, but one of Oona's greatest dreams was to step aboard her father's ship. She didn't have to sail on it. She just wanted to see what it felt like to stand on the wooden deck and look over the rails and pretend that it was ploughing through the sea. But she knew her father would never let her do that. One of his favourite sayings was, "A ship is no place for a lady."

The Britts sat at a table that looked out over Nordlor Harbour. As soon as they sat down a man came to serve them.

"Mornin' all," the man said with a nod. He wore a captain's hat with a golden anchor stitched into the front. It was frayed and faded, but the anchor still shone. His name was Arvid and he was the ship's former captain. "What can I get for you?"

While her family studied the menu, Oona looked around the room. She had been to the Rusted Anchor several times before, but today she spotted something new.

"You've got a stuffed cat." She nodded to the tavern's farthest corner where a tabby ginger cat with long whiskers stood frozen on a bronze statue base.

"Ah, old Mistress Bluebell," Arvid said fondly. "Went down with the ship and dredged back up with it too. The only soul we lost. She's got barnacles stuck to her fur and stinks like the deepest and darkest part of the sea. I've washed her eight hundred times, with soap and all. But I can't get the blasted stench out. I used to keep her in the kitchen, but her smell was leeching into the food. Smelled lovely when she was alive, she did." A smile branched across the former captain's face. "Like roses at dawn and fish pie at dusk. She would've loved this place." Tears shone in Arvid's eyes. "I named the pie after her. She loved pie, she did. Snapper. Seal. Whale. Any type of pie. You just had to put pastry on the base, gravy in the middle and a lid on top and she'd eat it."

"Enough about blasted cats," Oona's father said. "Let's order."

"But don't you like your cat?" Oona asked. She would give anything to have a real cat of her own, even just a land one.

"You mean Barnacles?" her father said. "I would have thrown him overboard years ago, but the darn thing's too fast to catch."

"I wouldn't go doing that, Captain Britt," Arvid said. "I've never heard of a ship without a cat. Be bad luck, that would. Put a curse on the whole vessel."

"Well, having a cat on yours certainly didn't stop it from sinking. Now. . ." Oona's father glanced at the menu. "I'll have the reindeer steak with cabbage on the side."

When it came time for Oona to order she said, "I think I'll have Mistress Bluebell's pie."

Oona had almost finished her pie when her mother and father revealed the reason for the lunch.

"As you know," their mother said, "your father heads north in a few months for the Great Hunt. And this year, we're going to set off on an adventure of our own."

At the word "adventure" – a word that had never left her mother's mouth before – Oona's face lit up.

"We're going north?" Oona couldn't believe it. One of her greatest dreams was coming true.

Around the table, Oona's sisters reeled back with horror.

"It's not true, is it, Mother?" Ina said. "You're not making us go up there. Are you?"

"Oh, please, Mother. No. Don't make us go," begged Berit. "It's dreadfully cold and the sea is so wet."

"I'm not going. I won't. I just *won't*, Mother," Sissel declared.

"We'll smell of fish," Trine said with a wrinkled nose.

"We'll die!" wailed Onka and Plonka. They threw their arms dramatically in the air. "We'll all just *die* if we go up there."

"Settle down, girls. Settle down," their mother said. "Of course we're not going north." She cast a dirty glance Oona's way. "We'd never do that to you."

Oona's sisters cried with relief, making such a mess that Arvid had to stop serving other customers and fetch a mop to clean the tears up.

"Then where are we going?" Oona asked when the floor was dry.

"While your father sails north," Oona's mother said. "We're going to go south."

"South?" Oona felt like she was going to vomit. Going south didn't sound like an adventure; it sounded like a nightmare. Nothing exciting ever happened down there. "What am I going to do in the South?"

"Why, you'll all get married," Oona's father said.

"Just like every girl dreams," her mother added. Tears of joy glistened in her blue eyes.

"Married?" Oona's jaw dropped. "But I'm only ten."

"Almost eleven," her father corrected. "That's when girls are allowed to marry down there."

"And you won't be expected to have children for at least two years," her mother offered.

"Children?" Oona's jaw dropped even lower. "But I don't want children. I want a cat."

"You can have mine," her father mumbled.

"Oh, hush," Oona's mother told her. "Don't speak of such things. Every girl wants to be a loving wife and a doting mother."

Around the table, six heads nodded in agreement. A seventh remained firmly still.

"But it's not fair," Oona said. "I don't want to go south. I want to stay here. Please, Father." She turned to the captain. "Can I stay here with you?"

The captain shook his head. "The North is no place for a lady."

"But . . . but. . ."

Around the table, Oona's sisters laughed.

"Why would you want to stay in the North," Ina said, "when the South is so much better?"

"It's warmer," Berit said.

"There are lots of handsome boys, who *don't* smell of fish," Sissel added.

"The cobbles aren't wet," Trine declared.

"There are princes in every town," Onka gushed.

"And," Plonka added, "the sun shines every day and it never gets dark, not even at night."

"Besides," Oona's mother said. "Why would you want to stay here? You don't even have any friends."

"Yeah," Ina said. "No one in the North likes you, not even us, and we're your family."

Oona wanted to say that Ina and her mother were wrong. But the truth was, they were right. She had never been liked or loved by anyone. She had no friends and she didn't feel like she belonged to her family. Even greater than her wish to go north, was her wish to be loved. And she wanted her father to love her most of all. It took her a long time to figure out why his love was so important. It was because she admired him. He was brave. He was successful. And he was the captain of his very own ship. Oona had a feeling that if she could be all those things, then he would love her too.

Freydis couldn't understand why the girl looked so sad. If she were eating a pie fresh from the oven, she would be ecstatic. She licked her lips at the thought. Back in the day she could have bought one hundred of them. Now, she couldn't even afford one. This was the third year in a row that she'd eaten all her meals from a bin. She used to live like a queen, she did, before that blasted fortune: the one that she got wrong.

Freydis stepped away from the window and shook her head. Captain Britt had wanted to tie her to the mast of his ship after that one. He had wanted to sail her into the Icelands and drop her into the sea. And it wasn't an empty threat either. A shell had whispered the same thing not four hours before Oona Britt was born. That's why she hadn't gone to the party at the Sinking Eel.

Just one word wrong, Freydis thought as she walked away from the Rusted Anchor. Just the one: boy instead of girl. What about all the other bits she got right? The captain's wife did give birth to a baby who grew to be bold and brave. His other six daughters were certainly disappointing. And – the biggest bit of all – she'd predicted the captain's wife was pregnant three months before she started showing!

But no. All anyone in Nordlor cared about was the boy bit. One word had ruined a thirty-year career. And word up here spread. The night Oona Britt was born, eighty sea robins were sent into the air. They flew to villages far and wide, carrying the same message: *Freydis Spits is a fraud.*

She, the Great Freydis Spits, a fraud? How dare they! Even now her cheeks flared red with rage. Her reputation had been ruined North-wide.

For years Freydis had wondered why the shell told her the wrong fortune. It had never happened to her before. After much deliberation, she had come to the only solution. She must have heard wrong. It was obvious to her now. She had heard the word "son" instead of "one". She wasn't losing her touch. She just needed to clean out her ears.

But even after Freydis cleaned out her ears, the people of Nordlor refused to buy any more fortunes. Slowly, her money had run out and she'd had to sell her carriage for food. That had been her second mistake. It was too dangerous to travel by foot in the North. Until she could afford a new carriage, or even just a horse, she couldn't go anywhere.

In protest at the unfairness of it all, Freydis had taken a vow of silence. She had not voiced a single prediction in almost ten years. That's right. She didn't tell anyone about the Sinking Eel burning down or the polar bear lying in wait to kill those five men in the woods.

Yes, Freydis Spits was a woman of principle. If no one cared to listen, then she would not speak.

But things were getting desperate. Eating out of bins. Washing in the fjord. Knitting winter clothes out of dead grass. This wasn't how a fortune teller was meant to live.

No. The time for silence had passed. Freydis Spits had to become a famed fortune teller once more, and there was only one way to do that. She had to find a shell with a future grand enough to sell.

THE WRECKAGE

Oona Britt liked a lot of things about Nordlor. She liked the way it always smelled of salty water and fresh fish. She liked the way the houses bobbed on the cobbles like they were made of waves instead of stone. And she liked the way the whole village seemed to freeze in winter. But the one thing in Nordlor that Oona liked most of all was school. Unfortunately for her, like most of the wonderful things in Nordlor, school was only for the boys.

Once, Oona had asked her mother if she could go to school as well. But her mother had just laughed and said, "Why would you want to learn things at school when men can explain everything for you?"

Oona could not understand her mother's logic regarding these things and nor did she want to. But luckily for her, she had discovered a way to overcome this obstacle all by herself.

In Nordlor, school was held every day from nine in the morning until one in the afternoon. Like most important gatherings, it took place in the village hall. And while everyone knew where the village hall was, only one person had discovered the hidden hole in the ceiling that led into the roof. It was through this space that Oona climbed every morning at eight. Then, for the next five hours, she would peer through a gap in the wood and watch the lessons below. In a way, it was lucky her family didn't care about her. Otherwise, they would have wondered what she got up to every day.

But even with a hidden spot in the roof, attending school wasn't an easy task. The ship that made the village hall had sunk amid a wild storm, and every day at eleven a monstrous gale ripped through the roof space. The wind roared so loudly that Oona could not hear a word from the classroom below until half past twelve in the afternoon. Luckily, Oona always brought a book along so she wouldn't get bored.

Oona owned two books: *The Twenty Greatest Shipwrecks in the North* and *Great Northern Sea Tales*. She had not bought the books herself, nor had she written them. Instead, they had been given to her. The only problem was, Oona didn't know who by. It was the one great mystery in her life.

Every year on Oona's birthday she would awake to find a present on her window sill. The present would be wrapped in brown paper and tied together with sailor's string. But there would never be a card, so she did not know who had sent it.

For the last ten years this stranger had given her birthday presents, and they always got her the right thing. So far she had received a knitted blanket with her initials "OB" hand-stitched into the side; several toys, including a miniature whaleboat that could float on the river just like a real one; an abacus made of seashells; a bag of sweets shaped like the greatest whaling ships in the North; a small wooden sea chest; two books, one about shipwrecks followed the next year by one full of sea tales; and, just this year past, she had received her knitted cat, Gillbert.

Oona knew the presents weren't from her sisters

or her parents. They never gave her anything nice. In fact, some years they didn't give her anything at all. So, they must have been from someone else. But who?

Oona had tried to find out their identity. One year she had dusted salt on her window sill. In the morning she had found the imprint of a hand on top. But it was smeared so much she couldn't even make out the fingerprints let alone use them to find out who the hand had belonged to. Another year, she set a trap with sailor's string. She tied one end of the string across the outside of the window and the other end to her wrist. The plan had been for her to wake up when the stranger accidentally pressed against the string. But the stranger must have seen it, for, in the morning the string was still there, untouched, while a new present sat beside it.

When her second idea failed, Oona tried a third. If she couldn't wake up when the stranger arrived, she would have to stay awake all night. The plan had been going well. Midnight had passed and she had still been awake. But then she had started to yawn and her eyes had grown heavy. She stayed awake until one in the morning, but by two she was fast asleep. Oona awoke just before dawn to the sight of Gillbert sitting on her window sill. She had raced over to the window and peered outside just in time to see the glint of a ladder in the moonlight and the shadow of someone carrying it.

The shadow had looked small, and Oona wondered who it belonged to. Had it belonged to one of the boys at school or perhaps to another girl? This possibility made her very excited: she'd never had a friend her own age before.

Oona wondered what present the stranger would give her this year. But then she realized something. By the time she turned eleven she would be in the South. Whoever the stranger was, she doubted they would find her all the way down there.

At the thought of never receiving another present from her secret friend, Oona's heart sank. She had hoped to receive a third book this year – perhaps one about sea cats or famous captains. But she knew she should just be grateful for the two books she already had. After all, without them she wouldn't have any, and her knowledge of this world would have come entirely from Nordlor itself.

Two days after learning she was going south, Oona had snuck into the roof of the village hall for another day of learning. But before the lesson began, shouting came from below. Only the shouts

weren't coming from inside. They were coming from the street beyond.

Oona peered through one of the wooden roof tiles. Outside a crowd had gathered and was marching towards the river. They were all chattering about the same thing: a shipwreck had washed up in Nordlor Harbour.

Oona raced through the lanes of Nordlor. The sea cobbles that lined the village glistened blue and then green and then silver beneath her feet. Even through the soles of her shoes the cobbles felt wet, like they had just been dredged out of the sea. Oona had to tread lightly or else she might have slipped. To Oona, it felt like she was walking on top of the ocean. It was the closest she had ever been to the Northern Sea.

When Oona reached Nordlor Harbour she pulled herself to a stop and stared up, in awe, at the skeleton of a vast ship.

Oona had never seen a shipwreck before. She had only ever seen broken ships that had already been pulled apart and built back up into something new.

The sea currents had pushed the ship on to Nordlor's shore. Despite all the water that had seeped

out of it, the ship looked soggy, like the weight of the entire ocean weighed it down. Every section of wood was charred black. Oona thought a fire must have destroyed it, but then she saw the holes.

Eight holes, each one perfectly round and larger than a man, were ripped into the hull.

"It's not natural," a sailor standing near Oona said. "No storm could create holes that shape."

Oona's eyes moved from the holes dotting the hull to the deck of the ship. Despite the charred wood, she could still make out the smooth curve of the rails, the roof of the bridge and the distinct shape of a small seagull carved into the bow. The seagull's wings were outstretched, like it had been frozen and encased in wood at the exact moment it took flight. Oona recognized the statue. She had seen a sketch of it in one of her books: the one about the greatest shipwrecks. This must be the *Gandering Gull*.

At the same time Oona recognized the ship, so too did several people around her. Within seconds, everyone was shouting or talking or whispering about the *Gandering Gull*.

"It's the eighth greatest shipwreck of all time," someone said. They must have owned a copy of the same book as Oona.

"It disappeared without a trace fifty years ago, in the coldest winter ever recorded in the North," said another. "It was sighted by another ship as it passed Fisherman's Hell. Then, it was never seen again."

"It was built right here in Nordlor," said a third person. He was an old man – one of the oldest in the village. "I remember watching it set sail for the first time, and also for the last."

"I always thought the men froze in their sleep," said a woman. Tears shone in her eyes; her father had been a member of the crew. "But, alas, they must have burned instead."

Talk of what had sunk the *Gandering Gull* soon turned to talk of what it could be taken apart and rebuilt into.

"My workshop's getting old," yelled a man standing near the stern. "Maybe I could build a new one."

"I've always wanted a second bakery," said Mister Blom greedily.

"You can have the hull and the deck for your bakery," offered Mister Bjorkman. "But can I have the mast for my tower?"

"Of course not," snapped Lady Summer. "You've already got fifty masts. Besides, I need the wood – deck, hull, mast and bridge – to build a summerhouse. They're all the rage down south."

Though she did not say anything, Oona knew what she would turn the ship into. If she could have it her way, the *Gandering Gull* would not be broken apart and built back up into something new. It would be restored, so the great ship could sail upon the Northern Sea once more. And maybe, just perhaps, she could captain the ship herself!

Hours after the crowd dispersed and all the people of Nordlor were lying tucked up in their warm beds, a thin cat left one ship and sauntered towards another. The cat was called Barnacles and he hated walking on land almost as much as land cats hated swimming in water. But he kept going, for he had somewhere important to be.

When Barnacles reached the wreckage of the *Gandering Gull* he stopped walking and sat down. The blue waves that crashed inside his eyes stilled and, for a moment, he looked just like a land cat. He let out a sad meow and stared mournfully at the broken ship.

Barnacles knew the ship well. After all, it used to be his own. He had sailed on it for eighteen years before it was destroyed. He still couldn't remember what had sunk it. All he could recall was being hit on the head with something hot and heavy at dawn. When he next awoke it was night-time and he stood on the bridge of a newly built ship in Whitlock.

That's how things worked in the North. Every sea cat had nine lives and lived them on nine ships. They didn't really have a particular role on their ships. They were more like a mascot – a good-luck charm – that made sure the ships returned home after months at sea. The *Gandering Gull* had been Barnacles' seventh ship; the *Plucky Leopard* was his ninth. He really did not want her to sink. When she did, that would be it. All his lives would end, and he would never rise to sail upon the Northern Sea again.

Two months had passed since he last went to sea on the *Plucky Leopard*. Barnacles loved the ship itself, but he didn't love the captain. In fact, Barnacles hated Captain Britt almost as much as the captain hated him. It wasn't normal; captains usually loved their sea cats. But Captain Britt treated Barnacles like he wanted to steal the ship, not keep it safe. He didn't seem to understand that sea cats weren't like humans. They didn't want to captain their own ship or command their own crew. They just wanted the privilege of sailing on the ship: the thrill of being on the Northern Sea.

Despite the way the captain treated him, Barnacles sure missed sailing on the *Plucky Leopard*. He missed the feeling of ocean frost dotting his whiskers in the morning. He missed standing on the bow as the ship ploughed through the icy water. He missed the sound of arctic gulls squawking in the air and then squealing as he sliced at them with his paw. He never ate them, of course. He only ate things with fins or scales. Yes. A fine sea bass drizzled with butter. A plump cod roasted on an open fire. Or a pawful of fresh arctic clams.

Barnacles purred and licked his whiskers. Then, his thoughts returned to the ship before him. He had loved the time he spent on board the *Gandering Gull*. It was the best crew he had ever sailed with, and the captain had been the kindest man he had ever met. Barnacles hoped that somehow the men had survived. But, looking at the holes ripped into the hull and the burned and twisted wood, he knew deep down that on the day it sank he hadn't been the only one to drown.

THE STORY OF THE NARDOOS

As the richest man in Nordlor, Oona's father could afford the most expensive house. Located at 31, Whalebone Lane, it was three storeys high and towered over all the homes around it. Each floor was built from a different ship: the *Sea Deer*, the *Crustacean* and the *Limping Lynx*. Yet despite the vast size of the place she called home, Oona lived in the cramped and dusty attic.

Oona's parents said it was because they had no spare rooms. But Oona had seen the empty room on the third floor. It was painted blue and had eight round windows that looked north, right along the fjord that led to the Northern Sea. When Oona had asked if she could have that room, her parents had told her it was a guest room, even though no guest had ever stayed in it. But still, she couldn't complain too much. After all, her attic also had a window, and if she pressed her nose right up against the cold glass she could glimpse the main square and the dock that held her father's ship.

The day after the *Gandering Gull* washed into Nordlor, Oona found herself sitting beside this very window reading one of her books. School had been cancelled for the day and she wanted to keep herself occupied.

At first Oona read about the disappearance of the *Gandering Gull*. But then she was drawn to her second book. For hours she became lost amongst the tales inked inside: tales of giant, magical creatures that called the North home. She read about the nasty kraken that picked ships up in the air and crushed them into splinters. The giant cetus that could swallow an entire ship in one bite. And the cheeky trolls that stole ships when they docked in harbour. Soon, the entire day had passed and outside the moon was rising.

Oona lit a whale-wax candle and read the last

chapter of her book. It was about her favourite creature of all.

CHAPTER THIRTY-EIGHT
THE TALE OF THE NARDOOS

Thousands of years ago the entire world was covered in ice and everywhere was as cold as the North. Along with whales and fish and seals, creatures called nardoos lived in the sea. But the nardoos didn't just swim in the water. They made the water, they made the sky, they made the snow and they made the wind.

The nardoos were bigger than whales, brighter than the summer sun and kinder than the kindest man. They were gentle beasts that swam through the waters during the day and flew through the stars at night.

It is said that when they cried, the nardoo's tears floated up into the sky and became clouds that fell back down as rain. It is said that wherever they flew they left trails of brilliant lights behind. It is said they had the power to push away the stars with their fins and sweep away the moon with their tails. And when they swam the currents in the ocean changed. They were called the creatures of the North and they used to be as common as fish.

But times changed. Just like we hunt whales today, the men of the past hunted nardoos. They speared them with their swords, trapped them in their nets and hauled them out of the sea. Then, when they died, they turned them into soup.

To escape the men who hunted them, the nardoos fled north, taking the ice, the snow and the winter storms with them. Now, instead of saving people lost at sea, they hide from them. It's said that if they all die the ice will melt and flood the world. People will have to live on ships until the sun burns all the water away and then we will all burn too.

When Oona finished reading, not for the first time she wondered if the nardoos were real.

"They're probably just a story," Oona whispered to herself. Nothing like that could really exist. After all, nothing was bigger than a whale and no animal could fly as high as the moon. But, the Northern Lights were real. Oona had never seen them herself, but once she overheard a fisherman speaking about how he liked to fall asleep beneath them.

"They look like an artist has sneaked into the heavens and used the sky for a canvas," the man had said one night while he drank outside the Rusted Anchor. "Sometimes the lights are so bright and so big you forget they're half a moon away and reach out to touch them. But your fingers only close around empty air."

Once, in a moment of weakness, Oona had told Trine about the story and asked if she thought the creatures might be real: the rare and gentle nardoo, the wicked kraken and the giant cetus. But even she, by far the nicest of her six sisters, had just laughed. And then Oona's parents had laughed too, when Trine told them of the tale their youngest daughter believed.

"I'll tell you this," her father had said in one of the few moments he actually spoke to her. "I know those seas better than every man in the North. And there's no magic up there, just ice, fish and, if you're lucky, a few fat whales."

Maybe her father was right, Oona thought. Maybe there was no magic in the North, or anywhere in the world. But she really hoped there was. Because a world without magic would be a very dull world indeed.

At the same time Oona Britt was reading the story of the nardoos, Freydis Spits was wading gingerly into the icy water of Nordlor Harbour. Freydis hated this part of the job. Usually, the waves pushed the shells on to the shore and she just had to scoop them out of the sand. But sometimes, like tonight, the waters of the North stilled and she had to go into the sea to fetch them.

Freydis took a deep breath and stuck her head beneath the water. Her fingers closed around a shell and, shivering, she pulled her head back out. The stars in the sky glinted, like they were laughing. Freydis hoped this shell was the one. She held it to her ear and groaned. There were no whispers inside.

"Foxes and thunder!" Freydis cursed. She threw the shell back into the harbour. "I'll have to go in deeper." She took off her elk-skin cloak, laid it on the shore and dived into the water. She swam down to the bottom of the harbour and pushed her fingers through the sand. Just as she ran out of air, her hand closed around a large shell and her skin tingled.

Freydis kicked to the surface and swam to the shore. She raised the shell to her ear and her eyes lit up.

"Yes!" she said. "This will do. This will do nicely. I'm sure to fetch a whole gold crown for this."

Freydis threw on her cloak and raced towards the village square. For the first time in ten years, she had a future to sell.

That night, unaware of Freydis' latest fortune, the villagers of Nordlor dreamed of all sorts of wonderful things. In his tower, Mister Bjorkman dreamed of finding a mast so high that if he stood at the peak he could see all the way to the top of the world. In his cottage, Haroyld Nordstrom dreamed that the daughter he had lost was never lost at all. And in her home, Lady Summer dreamed of the roses and tulips that dotted the southern lane where she used to live. While most people dreamed of imaginary things or places and people who lived far, far away, one person dreamed of her sister who slept only one floor above.

When Trine was younger she had believed what her older sisters told her. She had believed it when they said Oona was stupid. She had believed it when they said Oona was unkind. And she had believed it when they said their father's bad temper was all Oona's fault. But as Trine had grown up, her thoughts had grown with her. She had begun to realize Oona wasn't so bad. In fact, there were a lot of things about Oona that Trine really liked.

Trine liked the way Oona spoke up for herself and told people how she felt. She liked the way Oona argued for what she believed in, like the time she asked the village elders if she could go to school. And she liked the way Oona tried new things, like the time she taught herself how to swim.

In Nordlor, no one jumped into the river, not for anything. Even in summer it was cold enough to turn you blue. But Oona had dived in over and over again, for weeks and weeks on end. Slowly, she had edged further away from the shore until she could float and then swim in water higher than herself.

Everyone in their family, and almost everyone in the village, had laughed as Oona jumped in and out of the river. But while her parents laughed and her sisters did too, Trine had stood there wishing she could be as brave and bold as Oona. But Trine doubted she could ever be that. She was too much like her older sisters.

AN EARLY WINTER

The following morning Oona awoke to the cries of a woman running up and down the lane outside screaming, "I've sold one. I've finally sold one!" By the time Oona got dressed and made it out the front door, the woman was gone. But her cries remained. Oona followed them through the winding lanes of Nordlor until she reached the main square. A crowd had gathered in its centre.

"What's happening?" Oona asked a woman in wolfskin standing at the back.

"Apparently, the captain's bought another fortune," the woman said without looking Oona's way. "I can't believe he did it. Not after what happened the first time. It was so embarrassing, and the whole village was there to see it." At that moment, the woman glanced at the child she spoke to and blushed. "Oh, sorry," she said. "I didn't realize it was you."

Leaving the woman in wolfskin behind, Oona made her way through the crowd. When she reached the front, her eyes fell upon Freydis Spits.

The once-famed fortune teller stood in the middle of Nordlor's main square. Her clothes were in tatters and her hair was a mess. The only thing that looked clean and new was a silver coin clutched triumphantly in her hand.

Freydis' benefactor stood beside her. Oona's father looked embarrassed, like he couldn't believe he had just purchased another fortune either. He hadn't intended to buy it, not until Freydis shared a bit of it for free. This fortune wasn't about a child – a boy who would never be – it was about his ship. What she had to say might save him and all of his men. Even if it turned out to be false, he couldn't take a risk that big.

"Go on," the captain growled impatiently as he glared at Freydis Spits. "Get on with it. Tell me what you've heard."

Even though the captain paid for the fortune, Freydis shared it with everyone. She coughed to clear her throat, stuffed the silver coin in the deepest fold of her rancid coat and yelled across the gathered crowd:

CAPTAIN BRITT,
GATHER YOUR MEN, PREPARE YOUR SHIP;
SET SAIL NOW OR FREEZE.
WINTER IS COMING EARLY THIS YEAR;
THE DEADLIEST; THE DARKEST AND THE COLDEST
WINTER IN FIFTY YEARS.

*

At first, no one believed Freydis Spits. After all, why should they? She had never voiced a true prediction in the village before. But then the signs of an early winter started to appear.

First the cobbles that lined Nordlor grew awfully cold for that time of year. Then, snow began to dust the rooftops in the village. Snow didn't normally appear for another two months. Three days later a flock of owls so large they turned the sky above Nordlor dark, flew south. They only left the North when they sensed danger on the wind.

While the village folk may have been able to

54

ignore Freydis Spits, they could not ignore this. The day after the owls turned Nordlor black, chaos erupted in the streets of the village. Though no one wanted to believe the fortune teller was right, they were now too afraid to doubt that she was wrong. Winter in the North was never kind, and if it came early it was sure to be a cruel one.

The *Gandering Gull* became old news as the village folk flooded the main square and stocked up on items for winter.

Padded coats sold out in ten minutes, pickled herring was gone in thirty and by the end of the first hour all the whale meat leftover from the previous winter was stacked neatly in the top of Mister Bjorkman's tower.

"I'll be able to sell it for ten times as much when winter hits," he gloated to Lady Summer as he raced off to buy five crates of reindeer jerky.

Even the store owners themselves were panicking. Before the crowds hit, Mister Blom the baker hid half of the day's bread out the back. And when he closed that night he shoved eight sacks of flour and another nine of grain beneath the bakery floor. Mister Enger the candlestick maker hid ten barrels of whale wax and one thousand yards of wick in his attic. And Mister Ritland the tanner nailed fifty-five coats to the walls of his home to insulate the rooms.

By the time evening fell every store in Nordlor had run out of stock and talk turned to where they could get more from. While some believed that robbery was the best option, others fought for a far more ethical solution. When the disagreements dissolved into fights that started in the taverns and spread out on to the streets, there was only one thing for it. The council of elders had to be called.

In Nordlor, important decisions were made by the ten most ancient men in the village. When they gathered it was called the Sitting of the Elders because they were all too old to stand.

Oona doubted this was the greatest way to solve problems. After all, half of the council members couldn't remember their own names, let alone the topics they debated. But Nordlor, in many ways, was a backward place: a place where tradition came before sense. And so, whenever important decisions were made, they were made by the council of elders.

The council ruled over decisions that affected the entire village. One time they sent all the children to Islo to protect them from an outbreak of plague and another time they closed the gates of Nordlor to keep an aurora of man-eating bears away. After the birth of Oona Britt, her father had tried to get the elders to banish Freydis from the village: they had the power to do that. But the elders refused. If they banished one person for upsetting another, soon there would be no one left. The only way someone could be banned from Nordlor was if they upset the entire populace.

When it wasn't used as a school house the village hall was used as the meeting place for the elders. Today, Oona's father was the guest of honour. The villagers weren't invited to the meeting, but Oona had sneaked into the roof before they gathered so she could watch.

"There's only one thing for it," an elder said after the topic of debate had been introduced. "The *Plucky Leopard* has to leave early. Otherwise it will never make it back before winter closes in. If that happens, the river to Nordlor will freeze over and we'll have no whale meat for food and no whale oil for light. We'll starve and die in the dark."

"But what if the darn woman's wrong?" Oona's father blustered from where he stood before the council. "What if we leave early and winter is just how it is every year? Me and my men will be stuck

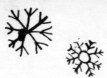

at sea for months before the whales return north after feeding season."

"It is possible that Freydis Spits is wrong," another of the elders said. "Though, she does have quite a good record with ships, Captain. Remember the whaler *Roe*? She saved it from sinking on its maiden trip."

"And what about the *Gandering Gull*?" said a third elder. "Strong currents must have carried it all the way down here. It's an omen, I tell you. It's an omen, you hear? An omen that come this winter we'll all be as dead as the poor men aboard that cursed ship."

Several of the elders murmured and nodded in agreement.

"Fine," Oona's father said. "Let's say the blasted woman is telling the truth. How long until I have to leave?"

The elders whispered amongst themselves for several minutes. Finally, they turned to the captain and one amongst them spoke.

"To be on the safe side you should leave within the week."

"*This* week?" the captain yelled. "But that's too soon."

Oona agreed. If her father sailed north this week then she and her six sisters would go south at the

same time. It wasn't fair. She was a northern girl, not a southern one.

But though Oona agreed with her father, it appeared none of the elders did.

"If you wait any longer you might be too late," one of them said.

"Your stubbornness will curse us all to death," agreed another.

"You are too young to remember what happened in the last deep winter," said a third. "But we are not. Two hundred men, women and children starved and froze and died in these streets. It was so dark that some bodies weren't found until spring. They looked as fresh as the day they fell. Nothing could survive in that cold, not even rot or mould. We lost half the village as we waited for the *Gandering Gull* to come back. But it took fifty years for that ship to return. If they had left this harbour only a few weeks earlier those two hundred people may have lived."

A silence fell over the hall as the elders remembered all those who lost their lives in the last Great Winter. Eventually, Oona's father broke the quiet.

"All right," he said with a resigned sigh. "I'll do as you say. The *Plucky Leopard* will set sail three days from today."

A LONG JOURNEY AHEAD

After the elders made their decision, preparation for the Britts' journey south sped up. To help them get ready, the family paid a visit to Lady Summer: the only woman from the South who now called Nordlor home. Lady Summer taught them all about southern customs, southern food and southern clothing.

According to Lady Summer, the styles in the South were very different to the styles in the North. Instead of dresses made of sealskin and thick coats made of fox fur, the dresses in the South were made of something lighter, called silk, and the shoes weren't made from wood and leather, but lace.

Lady Summer was very happy to help them prepare for their journey south. In fact, when they arrived she had everything ready, including seven pairs of southern dresses and seven pairs of matching shoes. To Oona, it looked like she had been preparing for their trip south longer than they had.

"It all seems a bit silly to me," Oona said as she and her six sisters tried on their southern shoes. "I mean, what's the point of wearing a dress that's so thin you can feel the wind through it? And these shoes." Oona lifted one of her feet. It was bound in thin white lace. "If you tread in a puddle they'll be ruined in an instant. And anyway," Oona continued, "why are we even going south? I mean, if the South is so great why did you come here?"

Oona turned to look at Lady Summer. As she did, her mother whacked her across the head with a shoe. Luckily, it too was made from lace, so Oona hardly felt a thing.

"Oh, do shut up, Oona," her mother snapped. "Lady Summer is a lady. You can't ask her things like that. It's not polite."

"No. No," Lady Summer said. "It's perfectly all

right." She turned from Missus Britt and looked down at her youngest daughter. "I left the South because I fell in love with a northern man. Unfortunately, he didn't fall in love with me. He left on a ship ten years ago – fled, I think is the correct term – and I've lived here alone ever since."

"Why didn't you go back home?" Oona asked.

"I didn't really like the South," Lady Summer admitted. "It's not the nicest place in the world. Most of the time it's far too hot and there isn't as much food as you would think. At least, not much food for—"

"Well, I think that's enough for today," Missus Britt said loudly. She feared that if Lady Summer spoke ill of the South, none of her daughters would want to leave. And that would make the captain very angry. "Don't worry about us. We know what we're doing. You've never seen true winter before, not like the one that's coming. Mark my words, Lady Summer, in two months' time you'll be wishing you never left the South."

While the Britts may have organized their outfits for the South, thanks to Freydis' latest fortune, they did not have a way to get there. Their father had originally ordered a handmade carriage from

Iceblown Harbour. It was going to be made from golden oak: a very rare and expensive wood that was as light as a feather. It came from a place further south than the South itself. A golden oak carriage would get them out of Nordlor four times quicker than one made from northern wood. But the carriage wouldn't be ready for months, so the captain had to come up with another idea.

"Are you sure this is the right one?" Oona's mother asked the shopkeeper. Her husband had sent her to the shop this morning to purchase something very specific. Her seven daughters stood around her, eyeing this "something" suspiciously. "It doesn't look how I remember."

"Indeed, it is, Missus Britt," the man replied. "Freydis Spits' old carriage – the grandest carriage in the North. I've had a lot of offers for this one."

While the shopkeeper may not have sold Freydis Spits' old carriage, he had sold everything that used to adorn it. Jewels had been hacked out. Golden whales had been pulled free. Even the old wheels had been sold and replaced with plain wooden ones. And they weren't golden oak. They looked like cheap birch.

"Oh, Mother," Ina said, "it looks so common."

"And old," added Berit.

"We can't go south in that," Trine said.

"It's embarrassing," Sissel agreed.

"Can't we take something else?" begged the twins.

"That would be preferable," their mother said as she continued to eye the derelict carriage. "Do you have any other ones?" she asked the shopkeeper. "Perhaps a golden one or even silver would do." If she wanted her daughters to marry southern princes they would have to make a good first impression. They needed something grand for their entrance to the South.

"I'm afraid not," the shopkeeper said. "Carriages are a rare thing in the North, even the plain wooden ones."

"Maybe we should just stay here," Oona said.

"I so wish you wouldn't talk," Oona's mother hissed. "You say such silly things. Don't mind her, Mister Opsal. Not right in the head. Not like my other daughters." She smiled fondly at the older ones and then made up her mind. "If we want to go south before winter we will have to take this carriage. But don't worry, girls. We can fancy it up. By tomorrow it will look even grander than when it was first built."

Despite their mother's optimism, none of her daughters looked convinced.

"Now," Missus Britt said, "you don't happen to have the polar bears, do you?"

"Ran for the hills nine years ago," the shopkeeper said. "Right after I sold their chains to a collector in the South. Haven't been spotted since. I do have two horses though."

"Horses will have to do," their mother said with a disappointed sigh. What an entrance they would have made with four polar bears. She bet no one in the South had ever seen one before. "We will, of course, need a driver, preferably one who can read. Could you take us?"

The shopkeeper was about to say no, but then he remembered the previous carriage owner's prediction. This might be his only chance to escape the impending winter. "I could ... for a price," he said.

When a price had been agreed – for the carriage, horses and driver – Missus Britt made one final request. "Could we have the carriage delivered to our house by noon? We'll need time to do it up before we leave."

Oona's six sisters were even more excited about dressing up the carriage than dressing up themselves. They spent all afternoon gluing jewels to its walls, tying lace to the windows and arranging pillows in the cabin. They even found some gold glitter and dusted it over the wheels. When evening fell, the carriage shone gaudily in the moonlight.

"Oh, doesn't it look wonderful?" Missus Britt exclaimed when her daughters revealed the newly transformed carriage.

"Delightful," her husband said dryly. He had left his study to examine the carriage he had purchased for ten golden crowns. He could have bought a small boat for the same price. "I hope you're going to fix that back wheel." He pointed to the left one which was hanging off at a very odd angle. "Wouldn't want to lose one along the way."

"Oh, forget the wheels," his wife said, "and look at the lace. We'll have the finest carriage in all of the South."

From where she stood beside her father, Oona snorted. She thought the carriage looked even cheaper than when they had bought it that morning.

"Stop being so negative, Oona," her mother said. "Your sisters have been working on this all afternoon, which is more than I can say for you. What have you been doing today?"

"She was probably playing down by the harbour," Ina said. "That's where we found her the other day."

"Yeah," Berit agreed. "She was probably down there playing with her stupid stuffed cat."

"How could I be playing with Gillbert," Oona said, "when you threw him in the water?"

At the memory, Oona's sisters laughed. Out of the corner of her eye, Oona saw her mother and father laughing too.

"You really are too old to be playing with toys," Oona's mother said.

"I wasn't playing with toys," Oona replied. "I was reading." As soon as the last word left her mouth, Oona wished she could swallow it back up.

"Reading?" her mother said. "Where did you learn to do that?"

"Nowhere," Oona said quickly. Then, before her mother could ask any more questions, she spun on her heel and ran off down Whalebone Lane.

Oona ran down the glistening lanes of Nordlor. The waves trapped in the sea cobbles crashed beneath her. With only the moon lighting her way, she could not see very far ahead. So, even though her own legs carried her there, Oona was surprised when she reached Nordlor's shore.

Beneath the milky glow of the sky, Oona stared up at the skeleton of a vast and broken ship. The *Gandering Gull* looked lonely tonight. The news of an early winter had robbed everyone's attention, and the village folk had forgotten all about the ship they had waited half a century to return.

Oona had always wanted to board a ship. True, she had imagined that ship would be a bright, loud, bustling vessel heading off for the Great Northern Sea. But with only one day to go before she left for the South, she knew that would never happen. So, a cold, broken and silent ship would have to do.

Oona boarded the *Gandering Gull* through one of the eight holes that dotted its hull. Despite burning fifty years before, the ship still smelled of smoke, and far off in the distance, like it had to cross half a sea to reach her, Oona could just make out the sound of a fiddle being played and men cheering, "Encore! Encore!"

The sounds of the sea were so real it felt like Oona was sailing deep through the North, not standing on the shore of Nordlor. Even though she was on a black, broken and empty ship, she had never felt so alive. This was the place she was meant to be: on a ship, not inside an old and rickety carriage.

Apart from the memories held in the wood, there were no signs of life on board the old ship. But there were signs that men had once been there. Broken cutlery littered the floor, rags that had once been clothes hung from the walls and, if you looked closely, you could see two empty, rusted candlesticks lying on the floor.

Oona moved through the core of the ship until she reached the room where the men had slept. Bunks carved from wood lined the walls. Time and fire had made them weak and they crumbled at her touch.

The moonlight shining through the broken hull revealed a series of carvings etched above one of the beds. Oona traced her fingers along the images. Each one had a number engraved beneath it. There were drawings of whales being speared, fish being trapped in nets and a boat full of men being hauled on board. Oona realized the numbers were dates – they matched each year the ship went to sea – and the images recorded what happened.

Oona skimmed over the images until she reached the final one. The number beneath it matched the year that the ship disappeared. The final etching was of a fish swimming through the sky instead of the sea. Instead of fins, the fish had wings: great big ones that were wider than the ship itself. Oona recognized the creature. She had seen a drawing of it before in one of her books. It was a nardoo.

Oona's heart began to race. If all the etchings around the nardoo were real, then surely the last one was too. Not only that, the *Gandering Gull* itself was proof that something existed in the Northern Sea that wasn't normal. That wasn't natural. That's what the man standing near her had said when it first washed ashore. Whatever destroyed this ship had not been seen by any man before.

Oona walked over to one of the holes in the hull and looked up towards the sky. Tonight, she wasn't looking at the stars or the moon. She was looking past them, far off to the distant North. She wanted to see a hint, a glint, of rainbow in the sky. But from here in Nordlor the heavens looked black.

Oona realized that she would never see a nardoo in Nordlor. And there was no chance of seeing one in the South: the waters were too warm down there. There was only one way to see a nardoo for herself. She would have to sail north and find one.

A bigger warning not to go – a broken, sunken and lost ship – she could not find. Yet despite her fear of the dangers in the North, she was far more fearful of going south.

Oona stared up at the lonely moon. She knew what she had to do. Forget feeling the North in the tips of her toes. She was going to feel it all around. She wasn't going south, no matter what anyone said. She was going to go north, just like she'd always dreamed.

It was a big decision: four whole months at sea. It would be dangerous and wet. It would be cold and windy. And maybe she would fall overboard and drown. But it would, without a doubt, be an adventure, and she had always wanted to go on one of those.

THE STOWAWAY

That night, while her sisters packed for their trip south, Oona secretly packed for her own trip north. Silk dresses were replaced with thick coats, while lace shoes were cast aside in favour of fur lined boots. Oona crammed as much as she could into her bag, including her only two books. Then, when everything was ready, she hid her bag beneath her bed and waited for everyone to fall asleep. The *Plucky Leopard* sailed at dawn and she would have to sneak on board long before that.

*

All was still and silent at 31, Whalebone Lane when Oona Britt climbed out of bed, picked up her bag and headed for the stairs. She was almost at the back door when she heard footsteps behind her.

Oona turned around to see Trine standing in the shadows. The moonlight trickling in through a window made her skin look paler than normal.

"What are you doing here?" Oona whispered.

"I heard you on the stairs," Trine whispered back. She nodded towards Oona's bag and said, "Are you putting your things in the carriage?"

"Yes," Oona lied. "I don't want to run out of space." She was about to turn towards the back door when Trine saw the edge of a coat sticking out of her bag. Oona had packed so many things inside that she hadn't been able to close it. Beside the coat was the sole of a thick northern boot.

"Where are your lace shoes?" Trine said.

"Under my coat," Oona lied again. "I thought I should take some warm things in case it gets cold."

Trine looked between the bag and her younger sister. "I don't believe you," she said. "You're not coming in the carriage, are you? You're running away."

Oona was about to lie for a third time, but she didn't know what to say. All of her family knew she didn't want to go south, so it would make no sense for her to put her things in the carriage early.

"You're right," Oona said. "I'm not going south. I'm going north, with Father."

Trine's eyes grew wide with shock. "Father's letting you go on the *Plucky Leopard*?"

"Well, not exactly," Oona said. "He won't know I'm on there at the start, but when he finally sees me we'll be so far north he'll have to let me stay." As she watched her older sister process this, Oona had an idea. "Would you like to come too?"

For a moment, Trine looked like she was considering the offer. But then she shook her head. "I couldn't. I'd be too scared. I'm not as brave as you. And I can't swim either. What if I fell into the sea?"

"I'd save you," Oona said. "And I could teach you how to swim as well. It's not too hard, once you get the hang of it. I could even teach you how to tie sea knots. I learnt about them at school. The reef knot is my favourite. You use it for furling sails. And we could take turns keeping watch from the crow's nest. I'm very good at seeing things from far away. When Father's ship returns each year from the Hunt, I see it coming down the river almost an hour before everyone else."

Instead of reassuring Trine, this made her feel even more certain she was making the right choice by going south instead of north. She didn't know the first thing about sea knots and she had no idea what "furling" meant. Her eyesight wasn't too great either. While Oona was a true northern girl, Trine didn't think she was.

"I'm sorry," she said to her little sister. "But I can't go with you."

"That's OK," Oona said. Though, secretly she was disappointed. It would have been nice to have someone to go on the adventure with her.

"I'll miss you," Trine said.

"Really?" Oona asked.

"Of course. You're not like our other sisters. I think you're much nicer and cleverer too."

This time it was Oona's turn to look shocked. She wanted to ask Trine why she had waited so long to tell her this. But instead she said, "I'll miss you too."

Trine stepped closer to her younger sister and embraced her in a hug. It was the first time someone in her family had hugged Oona: the first time *anyone* had hugged her. It felt different, but nice. She hugged her sister back.

They stepped away from each other and Oona

carefully opened the back door. She was about to step out into the night when she thought of something.

"Trine?" she said, turning back to her sister. "Did you give me Gillbert as a birthday present?"

Trine frowned and said, "No. I thought you made him."

"Oh. Never mind." Oona waved a final goodbye to her sister and slipped out into the night.

The air in Nordlor was so cold that the sea cobbles had frozen over and the waves trapped inside were still. Even the stars in the sky looked frozen and did not twinkle as Oona walked beneath them.

At first the village was quiet, but as Oona neared the dock, yelling and singing drifted across the frosty air. Oona feared her father's men were already on the ship and her chance to sneak on board was lost. But then she saw the glow of lamplight inside the Rusted Anchor and realized the crew were having one final night of drinks.

The *Plucky Leopard* bobbed quietly beside the dock. Its name shone in gold across the starboard side. Lanterns flickered within the ship, but no sounds leaked out from the portholes. Oona stared up at the great whaler, took a deep breath and, for the

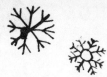

first time in her life, stepped on to her father's ship.

Even though Oona had watched the *Plucky Leopard* from Nordlor's shore for many years, the ship was a lot larger than she had imagined. The deck was longer than seven houses, the three masts that branched towards the stars were taller than every building in the village and the wooden rails were as high as her head.

Worried she might be seen, Oona climbed below deck. The ship looked just like the *Gandering Gull*, only an artist had sneaked on board and painted it back to life. Where there used to be darkness, light filled the rooms. Where there used to be black wood, polished brown now took its place. And where there used to be the smell of smoke and dank, mouldy cloth, now rose the smell of scented candles and fresh food, only just packed.

The first room Oona entered was long and thin and full of beds stacked against the walls. This was where the men slept. Behind her were two doors. A golden plaque on one door read *Captain* while a silver plaque on the other read *Navigator.* Oona knew what the roles meant. The captain ordered all the crew around and often owned the ship, while the navigator was skilled in reading maps and pointing the helmsman in the right direction.

Oona tried to open both doors, but they were locked. As she moved towards the back of the ship, she passed the mess hall, the galley and five empty rooms used to store fish and the innards of a single whale. Then she reached the final room before the ship gave way to the sea.

"This is perfect," Oona whispered as she stepped inside. The room was small and crammed with crates and sacks and bags full of food. No one would find her here, not for a long time yet. And she wouldn't go hungry. That's for sure.

Oona opened the nearest crate and peered inside. There was flour and sugar. Bilberry jam and salted elk. There was even her whole weight in cheese.

As she stared down at the food – there was enough to feed thirty men for six months – Oona smiled to herself. She couldn't believe how easy this had been. No one had seen a thing.

Barnacles had been sitting on the bridge when he first spotted the girl boarding his ship. He had been preening his fur. Once it had been a fine ginger with the longest strands of any cat at sea. Now, after two hundred years on the water, his fur was growing patchy and bald, with more grey hairs than ginger.

Barnacles knew the girl wasn't meant to be on board. He had checked the crew list only an hour before and there had been no females named. Besides, he didn't need a list to know that. The captain never let any women on board. It was an unwritten rule that had never been broken.

But this girl wasn't just any girl. He recognized her. She was one of the captain's daughters: the pretty one that didn't resemble a walrus. He had seen her countless times standing on land and peering up at the ship. A few times he'd even caught her peering up at him. But she hadn't been peering at him tonight. Not when she first climbed on board. Not when he watched her from the steps as she tried to prise open the captain's cabin. And not when he watched her snoop about in the storeroom. She was still there now, peering into the crates.

As Barnacles watched her exploring the food, the few hairs he still had stood on end. He did not care that the girl was a girl or that she was the captain's daughter. He cared that she was a stowaway. And if there was one thing Barnacles hated almost as much as one of his ships sinking, it was passengers who weren't on the crew list.

There were rules on a ship for a reason. If you didn't follow them, disaster could strike. He had learned this the hard way. When a ship sails in the Northern Sea, a lookout must always be posted in the crow's nest. This lookout changes every hour exactly on the hour. One night, on board the *Crackling Kraken*, a man named Einar missed the start of his shift by ten minutes. By the time he reached the deck the other lookout had fallen asleep, and by the time he reached the mast the ship had hit an iceberg.

Barnacles had lost his third life thanks to him. He'd lost his fifth life when another man on another of his ships – Erling the lazy cook – kept throwing fish guts into the hull instead of into the sea. Barnacles had meowed and hissed and jumped on the men, trying to point out the fish guts weighing them down. But no one listened. The ship slowly sank lower and lower into the sea until it couldn't rise back out. Water flooded the deck and then the rooms below. Some of the men escaped on the whaleboats, but Barnacles had gone down with the ship.

No, Barnacles thought to himself as he stared at the girl who had already broken three rules: no women on the ship, no stowaways, and no one allowed in the storeroom except for the cook. *This would not do.*

While all the other members of the crew had final drinks inside the Rusted Anchor, one man remained at home. Haroyld Nordstrom had been going to sea for over fifty years, but it never got any easier, not for him or for his wife.

"Oh, Haroyld," Mathilde said. "I wish you could stay here. Winters are always cold in Nordlor, and they're even colder without you." Despite voicing that she wanted her husband to stay, Mathilde was helping him to pack. He always left it until the night before he sailed.

"I'm sorry, Mathilde," Haroyld said, as he placed a box of ink and another of parchment inside his sea trunk. "I know you don't like staying here alone."

At the word "alone" Haroyld's eyes drifted to a cot in the corner. He had built it for a baby who never got the chance to sleep in it. Nora had been her name. And still, to this day, Haroyld could see her tiny, delicate face whenever he closed his eyes. Remaining in Nordlor would not have been half as hard for Mathilde if she had little Nora for company.

Thoughts of what he had lost in the past and what he might lose in the future, made Haroyld step back from his trunk. He looked around the cottage that had been their home for thirty years. He looked at the fireplace where he worked on his maps in the summer. He looked at the bed he shared with Mathilde. And he looked at the empty cot lying near the window.

Haroyld took a long, deep breath. Most of the men on the *Plucky Leopard* loved the smell of the sea. But when he sailed north, all he wanted to smell was the scent of home. He breathed in as much of the scent now as he could. He had a bad feeling about this trip – a feeling that, this time, he would not be coming back.

THE PLUCKY LEOPARD

The cry of an elk horn woke Oona up. The men were being called to sea. Oona heard the thud of footsteps as they stepped on board. Soon, dull voices joined them and one rose clear above the others.

"Prepare the deck!" Oona's father yelled. "Man the sails! Pull up anchor!" he cried across the morning air.

A trumpet of footsteps hurried across the deck. Oona heard a loud *thud* as the anchor was hauled in, and then the *Plucky Leopard* slowly lurched into motion. Sacks of flour and grain slid across the storeroom, and a crate full of fruit landed on Oona's foot. She cried out in pain. But luckily, the sounds above drowned out the sound from below, and the men continued to work.

Oona watched through the porthole as the village of Nordlor grew smaller. Soon it was dwarfed by the giant green hills that rose on either side and the river that passed through its centre. Then, at some point not long after they first set sail, Nordlor disappeared from her sight completely. Even though the village had been her home since birth, Oona didn't feel sad about leaving it behind. She felt excited.

Two hours after leaving Nordlor they passed the next village along: a place called Whitlock where the houses weren't made from broken ships but carved from white whalebone. Oona pressed her nose against the glass and watched it too fade from her sight and then disappear completely.

Oona continued to watch the world pass through the small porthole. The further north they sailed the smaller and wider apart the villages became. They sailed the whole of the first day and the whole of the first night. Then, for another of both.

The only sounds Oona heard as they moved

north were the waves crashing against the hull, the thud of feet up on deck, a cat scratching at the storeroom door and a fiddle playing at dinner. The only person she saw was a sweaty man who came into the storeroom to get supplies. Luckily, Oona was quick to hide and he didn't spot her.

On the third day, they passed Mournful Harbour: the last village before they entered the Northern Sea. Oona waited another two days until she was sure it was too late for the ship to turn back. Then, she pushed aside the bags of flour and dragged away the crates of fruit and went up on to the deck.

Oona stepped into the light. Gulls squawked overhead, but the sun made it too bright to see them. The air smelled of salt and fish. To Oona, it smelled like her father when he returned from his trips at sea, only stronger and wilder and fresher. Around her, the ocean stretched on and on. It was as clear as the sky; not an iceberg lay in sight.

Men bustled about on deck. They climbed the masts, they cast giant fishing nets into the sea and right in the centre of it all stood Oona's father on the bridge holding a golden wheel.

Oona had just spotted her father when a man spotted her.

"Oi!" the man yelled. "There be a lady on the ship!"

Every man on board stopped what they were doing and looked about them. Slowly, one by one, their eyes fell upon Oona.

Oona's father was the last man to see her. He left the bridge and walked towards his daughter. Used to being at sea, he crossed the deck as though he still stood on land. His steps were slow, but he reached his daughter quickly.

"Father," Oona said, looking up into his vast shadow. "I – um..." Oona searched for something to say, but all her words had dried up.

As he looked down at his daughter, the captain's face slowly turned red. He looked like a volcano about to explode. "What in the blasted sea are you doing here?" he thundered. "You're meant to be going south with your mother."

"I – I..." Oona continued to search for the right words. Unable to find them, she spoke the truth. "But I didn't want to go with her. I wanted to go north with you."

Oona had hoped her honesty would work: it would make her father see reason and let her come with them. But it had the opposite effect.

"Batten the hatches!" her father screamed. "Pull

in the nets!" he roared. "We're turning around. We're going back to port."

Oona couldn't believe her father was being so unreasonable. How dare he take her back to Nordlor? It wasn't fair! She bet if she was his son he wouldn't have a problem with her sneaking on board. In fact, she wouldn't have even had to sneak on board. He would have welcomed her with open arms and given her a private cabin.

Maybe she should have stayed below deck for a few more days. After her surprise appearance outside, her father had banished her back to the storeroom. When she'd refused to walk there, her father had picked her up – while she kicked and screamed to stay – and carried her down there himself.

Oona walked over to the porthole and peered outside. She wondered if this would be the farthest north she ever went. If it was, that wouldn't be so bad. At least she got to see the Northern Sea.

Oona had almost come to terms with returning to Nordlor, when she noticed something odd. The ship wasn't moving.

Oona poked her head out of the storeroom. Below deck was dark and empty. She hurried over to the stairs and climbed the first ten steps. She stopped just before her head appeared above deck. Her father was talking.

"She can't stay," her father said. "A ship is no place for a lady."

"We know you're angry," said another man. "But what's the harm in letting her come along?"

"She disobeyed me," her father said.

"That's what children do. They disobey their parents."

"I don't care what children do," her father said, his voice rising with anger. "I only care what they don't do, and they don't sneak on to ships when they're not supposed to and they don't—"

Oona realized too late that her father's voice had been growing steadily louder. Just as she went to duck below deck, a large hand reached into the shadows and hauled her into the light.

"Listen in on conversations they're not a part of!"

"Not a part of?" Oona said. "This whole conversation is about me. And I'm not going back." She folded her arms across her chest. "Not ever!"

Oona had hoped that by making a stand her father would listen. But he chose to ignore her instead. He looked past his daughter and to the men crowding the deck.

"Time to get to work, boys," he said. "If we move quickly, we'll only lose five days."

The men hurried to complete the captain's order, but one amongst them did not move.

"What are you doing, Haroyld?" Oona's father barked. "You heard me. Get to work. It's an order."

"I don't think this is a good idea," the man said. He had a warm, lined face and a white beard. He was by far the oldest man on the ship. Oona had seen the man in Nordlor many times, walking the streets with a kind old lady whose eyes sparkled blue like the Northern Sea, but she had never met him. "You heard what Freydis said."

"Yeah, well, that woman says a lot of things that turn out *not* to be true." The captain glanced Oona's way.

"But what if it does turn out to be true?" Haroyld said. "Even losing just one or two days could mean we all lose our lives."

A few of the crew standing nearest to Haroyld stopped what they were doing to listen. Nordlor was a small place – only two thousand people called it home – so Oona recognized the men and knew most of their names. She could see Peder: the father of a boy at school who always knew the answers. Over near the bridge stood Olaf the helmsman whose job it was to steer the ship. And up in the crow's nest keeping watch was Karl. He was her neighbour. Every morning at dawn he practised playing the dulcimer. It wasn't the nicest sound to wake up to, and Oona hoped he hadn't brought the instrument on board.

"Stop scaring the men," the captain said. "If the sea starts to freeze you can guide us around the ice."

"I can't guide the *Leopard* around the ice when the entire sea is ice. I know you are the captain and we will do what you tell us to do. And I know you like to gamble. But, please, don't gamble with our lives. What do you say, Captain? Can she stay?"

"We don't have any spare bunks," Oona's father said.

"She can stay in the storeroom. You're all right with that, aren't you?" Haroyld turned to Oona who nodded her head.

"I'll sleep on a sack of flour."

"That's the spirit!" Haroyld said with a smile and a glint in his eyes. He turned to the captain who still did not look convinced. "And she'll have to pull her weight," he said, "just like the men. She can get up at dawn and work right through to dusk to pay for her sneaky passage. What do you say,

Captain? Can we keep this ship on course? Can we continue to cut a passage north? Can we bring back a whale before winter closes in?"

"I can't believe it," Oona whispered to herself that night as the *Plucky Leopard* rolled about in the Northern Sea. Her father had let her stay. Her adventure started here. And she wasn't just going to find a nardoo. She was going to prove her father wrong. She would show him she was as good as any son he could have had. No. She would prove to him that she was even better. She would pull her weight, just like that old man said. She'd scale the masts. She'd catch the fish. She'd even turn the golden wheel if her father asked her to. She'd be the greatest sailor he'd ever seen. And it was all to start tomorrow!

POTS AND PANS AND BROKEN BROOMS

"The galley?" Oona said. "I have to work in the galley?"

"The galley is the heart of every ship," said Olf the cook. He was the man Oona had seen going in and out of the storeroom during her first five days below deck. So focused on the crates of food, he hadn't once glimpsed her hiding in the corner.

"But there must be a mistake." Oona didn't understand. "I can't stay down here. I've got to help. Pull my weight, just like all of the men."

"And you will," Olf said. He wore a white apron

stained blue with fish guts. His fingers were stained blue too. "You'll pull your weight down here in the galley with me."

Oona's cheeks reddened with anger. It wasn't fair. The other men got to work above deck. How was she going to see a nardoo all the way down here? The galley didn't even have a porthole. The only light came from a few spluttering candles made out of whale fat.

"Come on." Olf waved Oona further into the galley. "We've got a lot of work to do, and you've already put us behind."

"Behind?" Oona said. "How can we be behind? It's only just after dawn."

"When you work in the galley you have to be up two hours before everyone else. How else would we have time to prepare breakfast?"

Oona was so busy working in the galley that she did not get a spare moment to herself all day. While Olf the cook made her father a cup of tea, she deboned fifty fish for breakfast. Then, while the cook rested his feet, she cleaned the mess hall and scrubbed every pot and pan in the galley. She had only just put the final pan away when Olf told her it was time to start preparing lunch.

Oona had deboned another fifty fish for lunch and then cleaned the galley again. Afterwards, she was meant to have a few minutes free. But that was spoiled by a request, "straight from the captain's mouth," to sweep and mop the floors below deck. She had only just finished doing that when it was time to start work on dinner. If every day was like this, maybe she had made a mistake stowing away after all.

At dinner, Oona was not allowed to sit with the men. Instead, she stayed in the galley eating her dinner out of the bottom of a pan. In between bites, she would glance into the dining hall, and what she saw inside was very odd.

Though Oona had heard a person playing the fiddle every night since she'd come on board, nothing could have prepared her for the sight of who had been playing it.

It was tradition on board the *Plucky Leopard* for the cat to play a song for his dinner. Some lesser cats may have been insulted by this ritual, but not Barnacles. He loved playing the fiddle. In fact, he loved playing the instrument so much that it was he who had started the tradition all those decades before.

"Play us a song, Old Master Barnacles!" the men

cried as the cat sauntered towards the middle of the mess hall. He jumped on to a seat, plucked a few strings, then rose on to his back paws and started to play. For Oona's first night in the galley he chose a well-known tune: "The Coasts of the Northern Sea".

As she listened to the jolly sea shanty roll into the galley and trickle out into the starlit night, Oona couldn't hide her shock. She had, of course, heard about the famed polar bear in Islo who had been trained from a cub to play the drums and the arctic fox who could play the dulcimer, but never in her life had she imagined she would see a cat who was self-taught to play the fiddle.

When the first song was over, the men yelled, "Encore! Encore!" And so, to the cat's great pleasure, he played a little bit more.

Oona did not get a chance to go up on deck until two hours after dinner. She walked to the front of the ship where the bow was breaking a path through the waves. She breathed in the fresh sea air. It was a pleasant change from the smell of sweat, whale oil and smoke below deck.

"Ah, I see you've finally escaped the galley," said a voice from behind her.

Oona spun around and saw the kind old man who had convinced her father to let her stay. A pipe poked out of his mouth and blue smoke drifted up towards the stars. Barnacles the cat was rubbing against the old man's leg. When Barnacles saw Oona watching him, he hissed and ran over to the bridge where Olaf stood steering the ship.

"Don't mind him," the old man said, nodding towards the cat. "Takes about a decade to warm up to anyone. Haroyld Nordstrom's the name. Pleased to make your acquaintance." The old man held out his hand and Oona shook it. Despite the frosty night, his skin was warm.

"Are you a fisherman?" Oona asked.

Haroyld laughed so loudly his pipe almost fell overboard. "Never in my life have I caught a fish," he said proudly.

"Then what do you do?"

"Why, I'm the navigator. Without me, this ship wouldn't go anywhere. Well, not anywhere it's meant to go. Here, look. I'll show you."

Haroyld pointed up towards the sky.

"There are billions of stars up there, Oona Britt. But you only need to know fifty-seven of them to find your way around the world. Celestial navigation it's called, and I think it's absolutely splendid."

Oona stared up at the sky. Out here on the water there were more stars than she could ever see on land.

"How do you know what stars to follow?" she said.

"By their shapes. You see that cluster of stars up there?" The navigator pointed into the inky sky. "That's a leopard seal. And that cluster there" – he pointed far off to their right – "is a bear. And just behind us should be – oh!"

"What's wrong?" Oona said.

"Those stars are missing tonight. It's a sneaky one, that nardoo." The navigator chuckled to himself. "Some nights it's there and other nights . . . well, it's like it has decided to fly away."

Oona looked up at the sky and wondered where the stars had gone.

"If I could teach you only one thing about navigating, Oona, it's this. Now listen closely. The leopard seal leads you north, the bear shows you to the east, the owl points west and if you follow the nardoo, why, it will take you all the way home."

Oona had spent many nights looking at the stars in Nordlor. But she hadn't realized they had names, and she didn't know they could guide you all the way around the world.

"Do you know," Haroyld said after he refilled his pipe. This time yellow smoke drifted up into the sky.

"In fifty years I've never let a ship hit anything. I'm pretty sure that's a record. And no ship I navigate has ever come close to an iceberg. I've got a knack for navigating around them. It's all in here." He tapped his pipe against his nose. "I can smell them on the air."

Oona was about to ask Haroyld what icebergs smelled like when her eyes caught sight of something in the sky. Up amongst the distant stars, there came a flash of rainbow.

"The Northern Lights," she said. It was just a tinkling to the north, but it was still the most beautiful thing she'd ever seen.

"You'll see more of them, no doubt," Haroyld said. "They grow bigger and brighter the further we head north."

"Really?" Oona's eyes lit with excitement. If that was true, she bet she'd see a nardoo. She could put up with the pots and pans and broken brooms that made it take twice as long to sweep the floor just as long as she got to see that.

"You really wanted to come," Haroyld said.

"Of course. Didn't you?"

"I used to have sea legs when I was younger, but now these old things—" Haroyld pointed to his legs. "Just yearn for dry land." He took another puff of his pipe and confided a secret to Oona. "This is my last trip north before I retire. Don't know what I'll do after that. But I'm looking forward to it very much. Perhaps even more so than my wife. She's been asking me to retire for thirty years. Truth is, I never thought I'd get to retire. Always imagined I'd drown at sea." Despite the thick coat he wore, the navigator shivered. "It's terribly dangerous on a whaler, even a whaler as fine as the *Leopard*. Let me tell you, Oona. If you think the air is cold, it's even worse down there." He pointed to the black water below. "The water in the North feels like ice and it cuts into you like a knife. They say that if you go far enough north, further than we've ever sailed, the water is cold enough to freeze your bones and dark enough to make you blind. They say, Oona Britt, that if you go far enough north even the whales freeze in the long, dark night."

This time, it was Oona who shivered. She'd always thought that being from the North somehow protected her from its dangers. But if whales could die in the Northern Sea, that meant she could die too. For the first time since leaving Nordlor, Oona Britt was afraid.

While the girl, the cat and the navigator were up on deck looking at the stars, the men of the *Plucky*

Leopard were nine feet below.

"Bets! Place your bets!" Olf the cook yelled. As soon as the girl had left the galley he had pulled out a large board and was now scribbling down numbers as quick as the men could yell them.

"Three weeks!" yelled one man before slapping six coppers on to the table.

"Three weeks for Anders!" Olf yelled back.

"I'll go with four!" yelled someone else. He was so confident he offered up a whole silver.

"Four and a half!" yelled one of the others.

"Five!" screamed another.

The men continued to place their bets until only one remained.

"Captain?" Olf said. "What about you?"

The captain looked down at what bets had already been placed: bets on how long his daughter would last. The men weren't betting on Oona drowning or dying. They were betting on how long before she asked to be put on a ship heading south instead of north: how long until she wanted the safety of solid ground beneath her feet instead of the wild, churning sea.

The captain studied the other bets and then drew a golden crown from his pocket. "Two," the captain said. "I bet she lasts two days."

A MAP OF THE NORTH

I t wasn't long before things went wrong for Oona Britt on board the *Plucky Leopard*. The morning after she met the navigator she awoke to find the door to the storeroom locked. She had to bang and yell for two hours before a crewman opened it. She was so late to the galley that Olf had to make breakfast by himself. Except for her father, she had never seen one man so angry.

"Fifty blasted fish I had to debone!" he yelled when Oona finally reached the galley. "I'm going to have fish guts under my nails for weeks."

Oona had wanted to say he still had fish guts

under his fingers from their first week at sea, but she decided against it.

The next day, when Oona sat down for lunch, she discovered a pile of fish bones in her soup. And they weren't the bones she had removed that morning. These bones were at least five days old. They were grey and green and slimy all over. If she hadn't spotted them she might have choked to death.

But the cruel tricks weren't over yet. The following morning when Oona went to put on her favourite coat she found eight holes cut into the sleeves. They were so large it took her three hours to sew them back up. And then, to top it all off, the morning after that she awoke to find a pile of hair beside her bed. During the night, someone had sneaked into the storeroom and cut off a chunk of her hair.

Oona wondered which of the men was behind it. She really hoped it wasn't her father. But surely he wouldn't do that. Would he?

While Oona spent her days below deck slaving away in the galley, at night she was free to go up and stand beneath the stars. The navigator would always be there too: his eyes locked on the sky as he plotted their course ahead.

One night he showed something special to Oona.

"Here." Haroyld patted the bench beside him. The smoke billowing out of his pipe was pink tonight. "Arctic strawberries. My favourite flavour," he explained to Oona when she asked.

Once Oona was sitting beside him, Haroyld reached into the inner pocket of his jacket and drew out a thick square of parchment. With Oona's help, he unfolded the paper and laid it out on the deck. They had to place buckets on each corner to stop the parchment flying away. The wind was gusty tonight and very warm. Despite the fortune teller's prediction, not a sign of winter was upon it.

The parchment held a great map. It was so large Oona could have used it for a blanket. Marks made from green and gold and silver ink were scattered all over the top. Oona had no idea what any of them meant.

"It's my map of the Northern Sea," Haroyld said. "I drew it myself. It's taken fifty years. Do you know where we are?"

Oona studied the map. Right at the base was the town of Mournful Harbour. She placed her hand on the ink that marked it and moved her finger north. Then, she stopped.

"Are we here?" she asked.

"Close." Haroyld gave an approving nod. "Very close." He pointed to a spot less than an inch north of Oona's finger. "We're just here."

Oona leant across the map. A great expanse of sea billowed out around them. A shiver ran down her spine. The waters were so vast that if something bad happened it could take weeks for another boat to reach them.

"Now, Oona," Haroyld said to the girl sitting beside him. "Every golden star you see on this map marks a place where a whale has been caught."

"The *Plucky Leopard* has caught that many whales?" Oona couldn't believe it. Thousands of gold stars dotted the map, all far further north than where they were.

"Lords and Ladies of the Sea, no!" Haroyld laughed. "This map has been made using hundreds of other maps. You see, twenty years ago I travelled to all the towns along the Northern Sea and sat down with their navigators. Then, together we shared the spots where whales have been caught. I even found some maps in an old chest at the back of the Sinking Eel not two nights before it burned down."

"Really?" Oona's interest in the map suddenly grew. She wondered if one of the stars secretly marked the spot where a nardoo had been sighted.

"You like maps?" Haroyld asked as he watched Oona's eyes race back and forth across the parchment.

"I think so," Oona said. Truth be told, this was the first map she had ever seen.

"Would you like me to show you some more when we get back to Nordlor?"

"More maps of the North?" Oona said. "Yes, please."

"And maps of the South and the East and the West. I'm a bit of a collector. Got maps of all the places that have ever been travelled to and even maps of empty spaces where no one has yet to go."

At this last bit of information, Oona's eyes widened with curiosity. "You mean, there are some places in the world where no human has ever been?"

"The world is a big place, Oona Britt. You could travel your whole life and not live to see it all."

"Is that so?" Oona said slowly. A glint of excitement shone in her eyes.

"Steady yourself, Oona," Haroyld said with a chesty cough. "You've got to finish one adventure before you start another."

*

Though Trine had known about Oona's journey north, it took her other five sisters three whole weeks to notice Oona was not with them.

"Where's Oona?" Sissel said as their carriage bounced and cluttered along the road. They had crossed the border into the South eight days ago, and the roads had been getting rockier ever since.

"Perhaps she is in the back with the trunks," Ina offered.

"Or perhaps she is up front with the horses," Berit sniggered.

"Only she isn't," Sissel said, pulling her wobbling head back into the carriage. She had just looked to the front of the carriage and to the back, and her younger sister was not there.

"I haven't seen her since we left Nordlor," Onka said.

"That's right," Plonka agreed. "Maybe she drowned in the harbour. She was always spending time down there. She probably jumped in and forgot to jump back out."

"Stupid girl," their mother said with a sad shake of her head. "Sea-squelch for brains, she has. The night she was born was the saddest night of my life. Your father's life too."

Oona's mother was still shaking her head when a

sea robin flew through the window of the carriage and smacked her in the face.

"Ah, here it is," she said when her nose had stopped bleeding. The robin had been dazed by the impact and was now lying on the floor of the carriage surrounded by seven pairs of smelly feet. "It's the map I ordered." She untied a piece of parchment from around the robin's leg and laid it across her lap. "Now, girls," she said, "where in the South should we go?"

Oona's sisters raced to their mother's side. The sudden redistribution in weight made the carriage veer sharply to the right. The horses let out a pained cry, but their driver kept the carriage upright.

"Um..." the girls said in a chorus. Though they looked at the map, they had no idea what it said. Unlike their youngest sister, none of them could read.

"Driver?" their mother yelled. "Pull over. We need your help."

The man did as he was bid. He turned the two horses off the main road and came over to the window. After two weeks on the road, most of the decorations added to the carriage were ruined. The lace curtains had torn, a few of the cushions had flown out the window and within a day of leaving Nordlor the glitter on the wheels had fallen off. Now, if anyone entered Nordlor from the south, they did so upon a path paved in glistening gold.

"Look at this map," Missus Britt said. She thrust the map in the man's face. "And choose some place nice."

"Er. . ." The driver looked confused. "I've never been south before, Missus Britt," he said. "How do I know if a place is nice?"

"By its name," the captain's wife said with a roll of her eyes. "Nice places have nice names. Now, choose one."

The man looked at the map and said, "Summer Land sounds nice."

"Ooh, I like the sound of that too," Missus Britt said. "Where is it?"

"Down here." The driver pointed to a spot right at the southern tip of the map.

"No. No." The captain's wife shook her head. "That won't do. It's too far away. Choose some place closer."

The driver studied the map again and pointed to a spot slightly higher. "How about Berry Hill?"

"I do love berries," Missus Britt said.

"But I hate berries, Mother," Sissel cried.

"Yes, we hate berries," her sisters agreed.

Their mother sighed and turned back to the driver. Without asking, he studied the map for a third time. Eventually, he spotted a place that he knew the Britt ladies would love.

"Princetown," he said. "That sounds like the right place, doesn't it? And it's only one week's ride away."

"Well, what are you waiting for?" Missus Britt said. She snatched the map off the driver and pushed him towards the reins. "Get a move on. Giddy the horses up. We don't have all day."

The driver jumped back into the front of the carriage and took hold of the reins. When the horses didn't move fast enough, Missus Britt stuck her foot out of the carriage and kicked one.

"Get a move on!" she cried. The sudden noise startled the sea robin and it shot up off the floor and flew out the window. Missus Britt smiled as it flew away. Things were going very well, very well indeed. A place called Princetown was sure to have a lot of princes. Her daughters would be able to have one each. They would all be married by the end of the week. And if her daughters married princes they would become princesses and that would make her a queen.

FISH BONES

Things weren't going well for those on board the *Plucky Leopard*. Despite Freydis' prediction, the weather held no signs of winter. If anything, the season resembled summer. No ship had ever left for the Great Hunt when it was this hot. At this rate, they would be bobbing in the ocean for an extra two months as they waited for winter to catch up.

But that wasn't the worst of it. Without knowing, one of the men had carried a sickness on board. On land the sickness had been a simple cold: the kind that spreads each year and then leaves without incident. But trapped in the sweltering heat below deck, the sickness had morphed into something far more sinister.

It started much the same as it did on land: with a cough and then a sniffle. If the coughs and sniffles didn't clear up in a day, the men were struck down with a fever. Soon, it wasn't just the ship that sweltered but also the men inside. The fever would burn hotter and hotter. The men would sweat and cry and scream in their sleep. Most would survive the first night, but if their body didn't cool they would not be strong enough to survive the second.

Along with the sickness, fear spread throughout the ship. Icebergs and whales weren't the only things that could sink a boat. Once, a sea sickness spread so quickly on board the *Frosted Deer* that it killed the entire crew in a day. Maureen the cat had to guide the ship back to harbour. The villagers only knew what had killed the crew because they were still lying dead in their bunks when Maureen put down anchor. It was the only time in history that a sea cat outlived the crew.

For the first time since she snuck on board, Oona was glad none of the men, apart from Haroyld, spoke to her. And she was also glad that she had to sleep alone in the storeroom. The less time she spent around the men, the less chance she had of falling sick.

Within two days, ten men had fallen ill. Three did not survive and were buried at sea. On the third day, Olf fell sick and it was up to Oona to run the galley. Her first task was to cook dinner. The menu said fish stew. Oona had never cooked fish stew before, but how hard could it be?

"Ugh!" One of the men in the mess hall spat out his soup and guzzled a cup full of water.

"What is this rubbish?" asked another. He pushed his bowl halfway across the table where it smashed into two others that had already been discarded.

"I thought women were meant to be good cooks," said a third as he glanced towards Oona, who was peering out from behind the galley door.

Even Haroyld looked disgusted by the meal, though he was trying his best not to show it.

Oona knew the soup hadn't looked great, but she had hoped it would taste OK once she added the salt. Her mother always added salt to her meals, and Oona's father gobbled them right up. So, what had she done wrong?

As the men continued to complain about the

meal, one amongst them coughed. With so many men confined to their quarters, it was easy to see the source of the cough. It was the captain.

The men sitting nearest to Oona's father quickly moved away. The captain coughed again. This time, louder than the first. Soon, a tumble of heavy coughs racked his chest. Then, the sound of coughing stopped. But something was wrong. The captain's face was growing red and he was grasping desperately at his neck.

"Oh, Lords and Ladies of the Sea!" one of the men yelled. "The captain – he ain't sick. He's chokin'." The man jumped to his feet, ran over to the captain and pounded him on the back.

The force of each blow made Captain Britt's eyes bulge. His face turned from red to a worrying shade of blue. All colour drained from his skin and he dropped to the floor with a heavy thud. The captain did not move.

A silence fell upon the ship. Even the sea outside stilled. Though they had already lost three men at sea, none of the crew were ready to lose the captain. What would they do without him?

While the men worried about losing their captain, Oona worried about losing her father. She didn't want him to die: not now, before he had seen all that she could do, and not ever. She wanted to save him. But while she may have taught herself how to swim and tie over one hundred types of sea knots, she had not taught herself how to save someone's life.

As some of the senior crew were plotting their own swift rise to captaincy, a cat stepped forward.

Barnacles brushed his tail against the navigator's leg and sauntered over to the captain. He pushed a furry paw into the captain's mouth and plucked out something small and white. Barnacles threw the object on the floor. He scratched the captain across the face, and Oona's father woke up.

"Captain!" one of the men cried. "You're alive!"

The captain slowly rose to his feet. It took a few minutes for his face to return to its normal shade. When it did, he leant down and picked up the object Barnacles had pulled from his throat.

"A fish bone?" the captain said. "A blasted fish bone! How in Fisherman's Hell did that get in there?" The captain's eyes turned to Oona.

"I – er ... I don't know," Oona said. She had checked the soup three times before sending it out to the men. Maybe she should have lit another candle to help her see. It was dark in the galley.

"What's wrong with you, girl?" her father yelled.

"I put you down in the galley because I thought even you couldn't stuff that up. But you can't even make a half-decent soup or debone a single fish!"

"I'm sorry," Oona said. "I didn't mean to hurt you. I must have been ... preoccupied."

"With what?" her father thundered. "You only have one job: to debone the blasted fish! Get out of my sight!" And then, he sent Oona to her room without dinner.

Even though Oona was banished to a room full of food she was too afraid to eat any. What if her father somehow found out and got even more angry? What would he do to her then? Lock her in the hull of the ship until they got home? Tie her to the highest mast and make her stay outside all night? Or maybe he would just throw her into the sea? Oona knew she was being dramatic – her father would never do that – but she still did not touch any of the items stored around her.

It wasn't hard for Oona to ignore the food. She wasn't very hungry. She had been so scared that her father would die and then so happy that he had lived. But her father had just been angry. She hadn't meant to hurt him. She had been trying to help.

118

To keep her mind occupied, Oona pulled out one of her books. She had been so busy since boarding the ship that she had not had time to do any reading. She hoped she hadn't forgotten how to do it. She was about to open the book when someone knocked on the storeroom door.

"Can I come in?" a man whispered from the other side. It was Haroyld the navigator.

"Of course," Oona said.

Haroyld opened the storeroom door and stepped inside. He held out his hand and opened it. On his palm lay two small rock cakes. "I thought you might be hungry."

"But won't you get in trouble?" Oona asked.

"What's your father going to do? Lock me in my room as well? If he did that, we'd probably hit an iceberg, or he'd steer us south instead of north. Now, here you go." He held the cakes out towards her. "My wife made them. Always bakes me a batch before I go to sea. Between you and me," he whispered, "she's a far better cook than Olf."

While Oona ate the cakes Haroyld kept an eye out from the door. She was just eating the crumbs that had fallen on her coat when the navigator spotted the book lying beside her.

"Which one is your favourite?" Haroyld asked,

nodding to the book. It was the one about northern sea tales.

"The one about the nardoos."

"Why, that's my favourite tale too."

"Have you ever seen one for real?" Oona asked.

The navigator shook his head. "But I did meet a man in the town of Islo who swore he saw one soaring over his ship and diving into the water on the other side. He said it was beautiful. No. That wasn't the word. Wonderful. No. That's not it either." Haroyld paused for a moment and closed his eyes. "Ah, *magical*. That's the one. The man said it was the most magical thing he'd ever seen."

Haroyld was about to retire to his cabin for the night when a rumble of thunder rolled across the ship. Through the porthole, Oona saw a bolt of lightning shoot down from the sky and electrify the water. Then, the *Plucky Leopard* tossed and turned violently in the sea.

"What's happening?" Oona asked.

"Just a little storm," Haroyld said. "Nothing to worry about. The *Leopard* has survived over one hundred of them. I'm sure she'll survive another."

Despite his own reassuring words, the navigator looked worried. Oona did too.

"Here," he said, sitting down on one of the

crates beside her. "I'll read you a story to help you fall asleep. By the time you wake up the storm will have passed and there will be clear skies ahead. Now, let's see." Haroyld took the book from Oona's hands and opened it to the last chapter. Then, he began to read.

"Thousands of years ago the entire world was covered in ice and everywhere was as cold as the North..."

By the time Haroyld reached the bit about the nardoos changing the currents in the sea, Oona was fast asleep. That night, instead of worrying that her father was angry with her, Oona dreamed that he was proud. He was proud because, while he had been hunting for a whale, Oona had found him a whole constellation of nardoos. The creatures had left the sea and flown above their ship. Their fins had been adorned with feathers that twinkled like stars, and when she and her father had looked up, the nardoos had smiled down at them.

A DEATH IN THE SOUTH

As the North prepared for one of the biggest storms in decades, the South prepared for a heatwave.

"I miss the snow," Ina whined as the carriage bounced along a dusty road. It was hot in the South, even hot at night.

"I miss the cold," Sissel said. The silk of her dress stuck to her skin like glue. She had never been so uncomfortable in her life.

"I miss silence," the driver mumbled from where he led the carriage. The Britt sisters and their mother had not stopped complaining since they left the North. Half of them even complained in their sleep. Just the night before he'd been woken by Missus Britt yelling, "She was meant to be a boy. She was meant to be a boy!"

"I miss Oona," Trine moaned.

A silence fell upon the carriage. All the Britt ladies looked at Trine like she was going mad. While they may have all missed the weather up north, it appeared only Trine missed their youngest sister.

"I mean," Trine hurried on, "I miss the darkness in winter that never lifts."

"Hush now, girls," their mother said. "Look. I think we're there." She pointed beyond the carriage window to a wooden sign that said *Welcome to Princetown*. While she couldn't read the sign herself, the last word looked very similar to the place the driver had pointed to on their map.

The driver led the horses off the main road and they plodded down a smaller one. Soon, buildings rose around them.

"Oh, Mother," Plonka said. "It's perfect."

The grass was green, the houses were made of new wood, not old planks that had been warped and swollen by the Northern Sea, and fragrant flowers bloomed everywhere. But when they reached the main square they found the buildings draped in black and people wailing and crying in the streets.

"What's going on?" their mother asked a woman from the window of the carriage. All the townsfolk, just like the buildings, were draped in black. It looked like the saddest market day the Britts had ever seen: like the stall owners sold tears and tales of sadness instead of wine and cheese.

"Haven't you heard?" the woman said between sobs. "The prince – he's dead!"

"Dead?" the captain's wife said. "But what about the others?"

"What others?" the southern woman asked.

"The other princes. There must be hundreds in Princetown."

"There was only one," the woman cloaked in black said. "And now—" She gasped. "There are none."

"No princes?" the Britt sisters cried in a chorus. Now in mourning themselves, they toppled out of the carriage and began to wail on the side of the road.

By this point a small crowd had gathered to see what the travellers wanted. Two women stepped forward and looked up at the captain's wife.

"Excuse me," one of them said. "I couldn't

help but notice, you look like you are from the North."

"Aye," the captain's wife said sadly as her daughters continued to wail behind her.

While the Britts may have been dressed in southern clothes, they could not mask their northern heritage. The southerners were tanned while the Britts were pale. The southerners had golden hair while the Britts had brown. And while the southerners walked gracefully, like they were floating on wind, the Britts plodded and clunked about like a drove of pigs moving through mud.

"Then perhaps you should go to Turnip Town," the southern woman said.

The Britt sisters stopped crying and glared at the woman who had made the suggestion.

"We can't go to Turnip Town," Ina snapped.

"Turnips are vegetables," Berit pointed out.

"And we hate vegetables!" Sissel cried.

"Yes. Vegetables are disgusting!" the remaining sisters yelled. And then they wailed even louder.

"Indeed they are," the southern woman agreed. "But along with turnips there is also a prince in Turnip Town, and I have a feeling he would like all of you very much."

"It's true," said the woman standing beside her. "You girls are just Prince Manfred's type."

"Really?" said the captain's wife. She stepped away from her daughters and closer to the southern ladies. "And this prince, tell me, is he rich?"

"Oh, yes," they both said at once. "One of the richest in the South. Rich off the sale of turnips."

"They're a delicacy down here," added a man from the middle of the crowd.

The captain's wife jumped with delight. "Don't worry, girls," she said. "I've found another one. A *richer* one. Come on. Back in the carriage. We're off to Turnip Town."

Freydis was fuming. The day was warm and she'd already had to take off her elk-skin cloak.

"So much for an early winter," she grumbled as she sifted through the shells on Nordlor's western shore. A fresh batch had blown in that morning. There must have been strong currents moving about in the Northern Sea.

It was the first day of winter and not a fleck of snow lay upon the hills. For the first time in twenty years winter was officially late. This fact had not gone unnoticed by the village folk.

"Ooh, fetch me another coat," Lars the butcher

said to Freydis as the village sweltered through its hottest autumn day in fifteen years.

"This sure is the warmest winter I've ever seen," said Arvid the cook. Mistress Bluebell was stinking something awful in the heat. He'd had to keep the portholes of his tavern open for three whole weeks just to keep the stench away.

"When is the snow going to fall?" Henrik whined. Since his tavern the Sinking Eel burned down, he had been forced to take up a new job. Now, instead of serving brew, he shovelled snow off the sea cobbles in winter. If the weather didn't take a turn soon, he would be forced to sell his belongings for food.

While some in the village were annoyed with Freydis Spits, others were angry. Wives cursed her for sending their husbands to sea early. Mothers wailed in fear that their sons would be taken by the sea. And children cried out at night for their fathers and screamed, "Why did that mean old lady make our papa leave?"

Usually Freydis would have been hurt by their words, but she had other things to worry about. This was the second prediction she had got wrong. Maybe she was losing her touch after all. Freydis' mother, Gerta, lost her gift to hear the

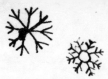

shells at eighty-six. Freydis was still thirty years off that, so surely that couldn't be the cause. Perhaps it was just another mistake. Everyone makes them.

While Freydis could dismiss one worry – the worry she had lost her gift – she couldn't dismiss another. The money she had received from the captain was swiftly running out. Soon she would be back to eating out of bins. And she shuddered to imagine what would happen when he returned from the Great Hunt. He had paid a whole silver for a prediction that wasn't true and set sail for a treacherous journey two months too early.

To take her mind off the captain's temper, Freydis reached into the sand and picked up another shell. This one was dull green on one side and sparkling blue on the other. She held it to her ear and listened to the words splashing about inside.

THE SEA IN THE NORTH WILL RISE AND ROAR;
BOATS WILL BE KNOCKED AND CAST ABOUT.
AND FOR ONE POOR SOUL ABOARD A WOODEN *LEOPARD*,
THE DAWNING OF A NEW DAY WILL SEE HIM DROWN.

Freydis' eyes flashed with glee. Though the future didn't say it specifically, she wondered if it would be the captain who drowned. She really hoped it was. If he died he wouldn't be able to get her in trouble for making another false prediction.

With this wish filling her heart, Freydis returned to the village and splurged on one of Mistress Bluebell's famous pies. Perhaps things were looking up after all.

MAN OVERBOARD!

Haroyld was wrong. When Oona awoke the following morning, the storm had not passed. In fact, it was just about to hit.

"Batten the hatches!" the captain yelled from the deck. "Tie down the whaleboats! It's going to be a big one, boys!"

Chaos erupted on board the *Plucky Leopard* as men raced to fulfil the captain's orders. Even the sick men were hauled up on deck and asked to help.

"You can die after the storm," Oona's father growled as he poked them with the end of a broom and herded them up the stairs. His recent brush with death in the mess hall had made him even more eager to avoid another, and he was sure to keep a good distance from them, even when they were up in the fresh air.

Only four souls stayed below deck. Haroyld could not navigate in a storm so he made himself comfortable in his cabin. Barnacles, not wanting to get wet, had joined him. And in the galley Oona and Olf prepared for the storm. They had been ordered to clear out anything that could spill or roll over as the storm tossed the ship about. First on the list were three buckets of fish guts.

"Up you go," Olf said to Oona. Despite his protestations about being too sick to help, the captain had forced him out of bed as well. Olf nodded towards the buckets. "They can't lift themselves."

"I don't think I can either," Oona said. The buckets were so heavy it took two hands to lift one.

As Oona struggled to lift the first bucket, Olf sighed and shook his head. "The storm will have passed before you finish. Here." He grabbed two of the buckets and left Oona to carry the third. "Hurry up. Hate storms. Worst thing about being at sea."

Oona and Olf left the galley and climbed the stairs. As they rose higher the wind howled like a pack of wolves above their heads. When they reached the deck, they found the wood covered in ice. As soon as they left the stairs their feet flew out from beneath them and they fell to the ground. A wave hit the starboard side and sent the ship veering sharply to the left. Oona and Olf slid across the deck. Oona grabbed hold of the rail, but Olf was not that quick.

The cook fell over the side of the *Plucky Leopard* and plummeted into the sea. The black, churning water swallowed him up.

"Olf?" Oona yelled. She looked over the rail. The cook was not there.

Oona spun around. Men crowded the deck, but because of the wind and the rain and the sleet and the waves they had not seen what had happened.

"Man overboard!" Oona yelled. "Man overboard!" she screamed. But the wind swallowed her cries and none of the men heard a thing.

Time was running out for Olf. Two more minutes in the sea and he would be dead. Oona knew what she had to do. She kicked off her shoes, jumped over the rail and dived into the sea.

The northern water felt like shards of ice cutting

into her skin. Oona sank down into the darkness. She feared she would fall until she reached the bottom of the ocean, but then her feet brushed against something hard. Olf was just beneath her.

Oona grabbed hold of Olf and kicked towards the surface. Just when the air in her lungs was about to run out, she broke through the water.

Oona gulped in fresh air. Beside her, Olf coughed and spluttered and splashed about.

While Oona and Olf were beneath the waves, one of the men had realized what had happened. A whaleboat had been lowered into the sea and now came towards them.

The rescue party picked up Olf first. Like a fish that had been caught, they hauled him out of the water. But as they reached for Oona a wave swallowed her up and crashed against the boat. When the sea settled, the men could not see her.

"She's gone," one of the crew said. "The sea has taken her."

"Almost four weeks she lasted," said another man. "I guess that means Morten won the bet."

"Not now, Lars," said a third man. Though none of them had wanted the girl on board, they hadn't wanted things to turn out like this. Ladies were supposed to die old and wrinkled and tucked up in their beds. They weren't meant to drown in the wild and icy Northern Sea. What was the captain going to think?

The men were about to return to the ship when they spotted something small bobbing in the water. They rowed closer. It was the captain's daughter. Her lips were blue, her skin was white and her eyes were closed. They reached into the water and hauled her into the whaleboat. The girl did not move.

A DREAM COME TRUE

Oona opened her eyes. She was lying in a room below deck. The room had all the comforts of home. There were cushions and plush rugs and blankets twice as thick as a man. Paintings of sea creatures adorned the walls, along with several giant bones that had once belonged to living fish.

No longer lying on a sack of flour in the storeroom, Oona was in a proper bed just like the ones they had on land. She had never been in this room before, but she knew which room it was. Only one room could hold items as grand and expensive as this. She was in her father's cabin.

Oona sat up and the world swam around her. She fell back into the bed and groaned. Her whole body ached. She had never felt so sick.

A warm hand touched Oona's forehead. Then, a voice asked if she was all right.

"Haroyld?" Oona said.

"Oona," the navigator replied. Relief softened his old face. "I thought we'd lost you."

Oona turned to the navigator. He was sitting in a chair beside the bed. A large piece of parchment was laid across his lap. It looked like he was drawing a new map. When he saw Oona looking at it, he quickly folded it away. "I better get your father," he said. "He asked to be told when you awoke."

The navigator left and five minutes later her father entered the cabin. He looked down at his daughter and shook his head.

"I thought you'd be dead by now," he said. "Didn't think either of you would survive the fall." He shook his head again. "That darn woman's predictions are starting to come true."

"How do you mean?" Oona asked.

"Look." The captain crossed his cabin and opened a porthole. Snow drifted down from the sky and melted into the sea. "The storm has passed and left true winter behind. And. . ." He looked down at his hands. They were trembling. "True, you're still a girl, Oona. But what you did was bold and brave. I'm proud of you."

"Really?" For her whole life Oona had hoped her father would say something nice to her, and now he had. She did not want this moment to end. Despite how frightened she had been diving into the sea and how close she had come to never getting back out, Oona thought it had all been worth it. Just to hear her father say those words. Just to hear her father say that he was proud. Even if she never got to see a nardoo, she thought that coming on this trip had changed her life in a way that staying in Nordlor never could have.

"If it wasn't for you, we would have lost another man to the sea. I don't know what we would have done without Olf. None of the other men can cook. And after tasting your stew, I don't think you can cook either." The captain laughed and then looked at his daughter. Suddenly, he grew serious. The next time he spoke, his voice shook. "We had to bury two more men while you were lying in here. The sickness still lingers. Truth be, I thought we would bury you too. But, look, you are still with us. And of that I'm glad. Now. . ." He coughed to clear

his throat. "Better let you rest. The quicker you get better the quicker I get my cabin back."

As her father turned to leave, Oona called him back.

"Father?" she said.

"Yes?" he asked.

"I can do so much more than you think I can. I could show you, if you gave me the chance."

"OK, Oona," her father said. "You will get a chance. Captain's promise."

With her father standing beside her, Oona smiled and closed her eyes. Within seconds she had fallen, exhausted, into a deep and contented sleep. For the first time in her life, her father was proud of her in real life, not just in a dream.

THE ICELANDS

Things on board the *Plucky Leopard* changed a lot after Oona saved Olf's life. After one last burial at sea, the sickness left, like the cold of winter had frightened it away. Oona remained in the captain's cabin for another three days before growing strong enough to venture beyond it.

The first place Oona went was the galley. But instead of having to make herself breakfast, Olf had made it for her. And she didn't even have to eat it crammed among all the pots and pans. Instead, the men had cleared a space for her in the mess hall so she could sit beside her father.

That's right. There was no more deboning fish for Oona Britt or endlessly polishing cutlery. Instead, she got to do all the tasks she had dreamed of doing when she first sneaked on board. She got to scale and furl the masts with her reef knots; she got to haul in the fish; and she got to keep watch from the crow's nest.

And that wasn't the best bit. For the first time since she had revealed herself to the men aboard the *Plucky Leopard*, they were kind to her. They taught her eight new types of sea knots; let her play Mattis, a card game full of tricks, with them in the evening; and taught her the words to shanties that were as old as the sea itself. For the first time since she snuck on board, Oona felt like she was finally one of the crew.

It wasn't only the crew who spent more time with Oona after she saved Olf. Her father also started to do activities with her as well.

While Oona had lain sick in his cabin, he had shown her all the things he had collected during his travels on the Northern Sea. He showed her a chest of whalebones, each bone almost as big as her. He showed her a rug made from the hides of forty-three reindeer that he bought from a tanner in Iceblown Harbour. And he showed her two paintings: one of a great battle between the North and the South and the other of a whaler hunting its terrified prey. The paintings were made by Henrik Holst, the most famous pigment artist in the North.

Oona had asked her father why he kept such precious and expensive things on board. "You'll lose them all if the ship sinks."

Her father's response had been curt. "This ship won't ever sink with me at the helm."

As soon as she was healthy enough to leave the captain's cabin, Oona's father took her to the bridge where he let her steer his ship. He showed her which of the seven handles to hold when she turned the wheel. He showed her how even the slightest touch could make the ship turn. And he showed her that when you spin the wheel towards the starboard side the ship turns to port.

Once Oona had the knack for steering, her father taught her how to fish. For days they stood at the back of the ship casting nets into the sea.

"We use small nets to catch fish," her father explained as he and Oona hauled one in. "But we use a giant one to catch a whale. It's so heavy you need eight men to lift it."

When Oona could fill a whole net with fish, her

father gave her a new job. Instead of deboning fish for breakfast she caught them instead. She was so good at catching fish she always had at least twenty left over, and it wasn't long before she had enough stored below deck to feed the village of Nordlor for the rest of winter.

Even though Oona was tired from working above deck all day with her father and his men, she always found time at night to look at the stars with Haroyld. By now the air was growing cold, even for the North. And sometimes, when the wind was still, you could see ice crystals hanging in the air.

"Blow me south and then north," Haroyld said as he and Oona stood shivering on the deck. "Freydis' prediction might come true after all."

Oona was about to ask what the cold would mean for their trip, when she saw something in the sea on the starboard side. The white waves of the ocean were crashing against something solid. It was a small island in the middle of the sea.

"What's that?" Oona asked Haroyld. She pointed off to the right. The navigator followed her finger and gasped.

"That can't be right," he said. "That's Fisherman's Hell. We can't be this far north already."

142

Though she had heard a lot of people mention Fisherman's Hell, Oona did not know what it was. She asked Haroyld to tell her.

"Some people think drowning in the sea is the worst thing that can happen to a man. But the sea can be far crueller than that. Sometimes, instead of taking a man, the sea breaks him. It doesn't happen often, but when it does it's awful."

"What does a broken man look like?" Oona asked.

"He does not look like a man," Haroyld replied. "And he does not think like a man either. He can't tell port from starboard, bow from stern or mast from deck. Sometimes, he can't even tell you his name."

At that moment, the wind changed direction and the sound of distant screams echoed across the deck. They were coming from the island.

"Fisherman's Hell is the place sailors go when they are not fit to return to land," Haroyld explained. "It's the place they go when they are broken and cannot be repaired. Once a man goes to Fisherman's Hell he never comes back. Even the people who drop them off at Fisherman's Hell won't step on to the island for fear of being trapped. They just throw the men overboard and the current drags them in. The currents around Fisherman's Hell never wash back out. If a ship gets too close it will be sucked in as well. The island is so powerful not even Hans Pilfer could escape."

"Hans Pilfer?" Oona said. She took her eyes away from the island and looked up at Haroyld. "Who's that?" She had never heard that name in any of her books or from spying on lessons at school.

"Hans Pilfer was a famous pirate who sailed the Northern Sea on the hunt for treasure instead of whales. And he found it. By the time he went missing he was one of the wealthiest men in the world."

When he saw the look of curiosity on Oona's face, Haroyld decided to tell her more about Hans Pilfer's disappearance.

"It's a well-known tale to men of my age," Haroyld said before he began the story.

The Golden Ingot *was the most beautiful ship that ever sailed. It was carved from golden oak – one of the rarest woods in all the South – and each mast was encrusted with glistening jewels. It's said that Hans built the ship himself. But most believe he stole it.*

That's all Hans Pilfer ever did. He stole from

castles, he stole from taverns, and, most of all, he stole from other ships. He was so good at stealing things that by the time he turned thirty he had robbed everything worth robbing in the North. So, in search of more treasure, he turned his golden wheel south.

Hans Pilfer stole from southern farmers; he stole from southern knights; and, he stole from southern princes. One day while robbing one of these princes, he came across a castle that was full of the grandest jewels he had ever seen. He stole a ruby necklace, a sapphire belt and a golden crown so heavy that if you wore it your feet sunk five inches into the ground.

Weighed down with this wondrous treasure, Hans and his crew boarded their ship and headed for home. But the Golden Ingot got caught in the midst of a wild storm. The heaving currents and the swirling winds took hold of the ship and carried it far beyond their home and deep into the North.

Hans didn't mind the detour. After all, he was still richer than he had ever been before. While his men led the ship back home, he opened bottle after bottle of his most expensive stolen wine and guzzled it down. By the time night fell he was stumbling about on the deck: ruby necklace around his neck, sapphire belt around his waist and golden crown atop his head. That's the last time he was ever seen. When the sun rose to greet the next day, Hans was gone. All that marked his exit was a broken piece of rail where he had slipped (or perhaps been pushed) and tumbled into the icy sea.

Ten years passed. No one heard a word from Hans Pilfer. Most presumed he died on the night he fell into the ocean. After all, wearing jewels like that he should have sunk straight to the bottom. But then, eleven years after he disappeared, a ruby necklace washed on to the shores of Iceblown Harbour. On each ruby was engraved a different letter. Together they spelled: "Help me. I'm on Fisherman's Hell."

A few men thought about going north to rescue him. But they feared the trip was too dangerous. After all, to get Hans Pilfer off Fisherman's Hell they would have to go there for themselves. The risk was too great. It was a fool's errand. No one would survive the trip.

Another two years passed. Then, one morning a sapphire belt washed up in Whitlock. Each sapphire was engraved with a different *word. Together, the sapphires spelled: "Whoever saves me gets the crown."*

This time temptation became too much. Men across the North, and a few from the South as well, boarded ships and set sail for Fisherman's Hell. Over one hundred men left in search of Hans Pilfer and his golden crown, but not a single one returned.

"That was over two hundred years ago," Haroyld said to Oona. "No one's been brave enough to sail there during my time, but if they did I bet you five silver crowns they wouldn't come back either."

A moment later the wind changed direction, and the cries from Fisherman's Hell faded away. Haroyld turned from the island and looked up at the stars. He studied the constellations twinkling above and shook his head.

"We are very far north," he said. "The storm must have strengthened the currents in the sea. We're two weeks ahead of where I thought we would be."

With Oona's help, Haroyld laid out his map. Then, using the stars as a guide, he traced his finger along the path they had already taken and stopped at the point where they currently were.

"Look here, Oona," he said. "Look where we almost are."

Oona peered over the navigator's shoulder and gasped. "The Icelands," she said. "They're just up ahead."

Haroyld nodded. "You won't know when we pass through, not at first. There's no fence or flag to mark its place. The water will just get slowly colder, the air as well, and instead of passing shards of ice we'll sail by chunks of ice as big as whales."

"When are we going to reach it?" Oona asked as she glanced between the navigator's map and the dark ocean stretching before them. Even when she first snuck on board the *Plucky Leopard* she hadn't felt this excited or frightened. She had almost died in the Northern Sea. What dangers would she encounter in the Icelands?

Haroyld glanced up at the stars and then back down. "According to my calculations, we'll reach the Icelands in about two hours."

While everyone else on board the *Plucky Leopard* slept, and Karl kept watch from the crow's nest, Oona and Haroyld stood at the bow and waited. If they had looked up, they would have seen Barnacles there too: sitting at the top of the highest mast, his blue eyes locked on the sea ahead. He never felt more free and alive than when one of his ships was ploughing through the Icelands.

"Have we reached it yet?" Oona asked. She stretched on to her tiptoes and peered towards the sea below. The water was calm tonight, almost like it was sleeping. The ship ploughed through it so easily it felt like they still stood on land.

Haroyld glanced at his map. "Almost," he said.

Oona asked if they had reached the Icelands fifteen more times before Haroyld changed his response from "almost" to "Yes!"

Oona climbed up on to the railing of the *Plucky Leopard* and peered down into the sea. Despite what Haroyld had said about not being able to spot a difference, Oona was certain more ice slushed in the waves below. And when she breathed in, the air smelled different. Not with a new scent, but like all the old scents were starting to freeze.

"That was just a lake before, Oona Britt. But this here—" Haroyld pointed his arms out towards the vast sea stretching before them. "This is the proper ocean. Forget fish. We're on the hunt for whales now."

*

While the girl, the cat and the navigator looked north, something in the water watched them. It had been a long time since this creature had seen a ship. After all, it had been asleep for fifty years; it only woke in the deep chill when a great winter hit.

The creature had been asleep for so long that the ocean floor had grown over the top of it. Now, clumps of rock were attached to its back. The weight was so great it had taken two weeks for the creature to rise to the surface. It had taken a further three weeks to find its prey.

Most animals in the Northern Sea survived off a diet of whales and fish. But not this creature. It had a far more limited diet. So limited, in fact, that it only ate one thing.

The creature could see two of these things right now, standing on the deck of the ship. By the size of the vessel, the creature knew there must be even more on board. It just had to wait for the right moment to get them. But it couldn't wait long. A hunger almost as deep as the ocean filled its body. If it didn't eat soon, it would fall into a sleep so heavy it would never awaken.

So, as the *Plucky Leopard* continued onwards, the monster of the deep followed it.

THE VERY GREEDY PRINCE

C aptain Britt's wife knew they had reached the town they sought when the horse stopped plodding forward and instead started to munch on a row of turnips lining the road.

"Keep going!" she yelled. She stuck her foot out of the carriage window and gave the horse a strong kick. "It's too far for us to walk from here." They were so far from the town they could not see a single dwelling.

The horse ignored the captain's wife and kept on eating. It didn't even stop when she climbed out of the carriage and whacked it with a handful of turnips.

"Stupid thing," Missus Britt hissed. "I wish the darn driver took you instead of the other one."

Two days prior, the driver, fed up with the whining of his passengers, had fled with one of the horses. He was going back north. Apparently, he preferred to brave the worst winter in fifty years than spend another day with them.

Missus Britt was still hitting the horse when a man yelled, "Thieves! Thieves in the northern paddock!"

Captain Britt's wife turned to see a short farmer running towards her. He was carrying a basket full of turnips and waving his arms wildly in the air.

"Be gone with you, thieves!" he yelled.

Captain Britt's wife had never been so offended. She, a thief? And to be accused by a farmer. How dare he say such a thing? People like him did not have the right.

When the farmer reached Captain Britt's wife he beat her with his basket. Turnips flew everywhere. The horse was so quick it gobbled most of them up before they hit the ground. The few which it missed soared through the window of the carriage and hit the Britt sisters on their heads. One even landed in Berit's mouth.

"Argh! Turnips!" they screamed. The girls ran out of the carriage and joined their mother on the roadside.

The farmer's eyes jumped with alarm. "More thieves!" he yelled. "More thieves in the northern paddock." When his basket grew empty, he leant down and pulled more turnips out of the ground. He threw them at the Britts as well. "I won't stop until you're gone," he warned. "And there are more than one thousand turnips in this field alone."

"Gone?" the captain's wife said as she dodged a particularly large turnip that had been aimed at her head. "We've come all this way to see the prince and we're not going to leave yet."

"Oh, I can take you to see the prince," the farmer said. "But he won't be at all pleased to see the likes of you. He hates stealing. He only has one place for thieves: in the cold dungeon beneath his castle."

The captain's wife turned as white as an iceberg. "Dungeon?" she said. "There's no need for that. We're not thieves. We can pay for all of the turnips, even the ones you threw at our heads." She stepped up into the carriage and returned a moment later holding a handful of silver coins.

The farmer stared at the coins and scratched his head. His hair was the colour of hay. "What's that?" he said.

"Money," the captain's wife replied.

153

"I don't think he's ever seen it before, Mother," one of her daughters said. And then all six of them sniggered.

"I have so," the farmer said. "Only I ain't never seen money like that."

"Oh, of course," the captain's wife said. With the threat of imprisonment looming over their heads, she had grown far more polite. "I bet you've never seen money from the North."

The farmer stopped gathering up turnips and stared at the ladies before him. His eyes grew bright with an idea.

"Did you say the *North*?" he said.

"Aye," the Britts replied.

"Is that where you're from?"

Again, the northerners nodded.

"We're from Nordlor," the captain's wife said proudly. "The Village of One Thousand Ships. You may have heard of it. And we've come all the way south so my six beautiful daughters can marry the princes of their dreams."

"Well, why didn't you say so?" Now, instead of picking up turnips to throw at them, the farmer was handing them turnips for free. "Wait here," he said. "Don't move an inch. I'll go and fetch the prince."

*

"Here he is," the farmer said proudly when he returned one hour later. He was smiling and did not seem to mind that the Britts' horse was still eating his turnips. "Prince Manfred of Turnip Town."

The six Britt sisters and their mother looked up at the prince. His hair was as black as the horse he rode, and he wore a cape of purple velvet so long that it looked like a dress. But their eyes did not remain locked on the prince. Instead, they were drawn to the thick golden chains that adorned his horse's neck. The chains were made of solid gold and glistened in the sun.

"Mother," Sissel said, tugging on her mother's dress, "Aren't they Freydis' old reigns?"

"Oh, hush, Sissel!" her mother hissed in a whisper. "Not now. The grown-ups are talking." She pushed her daughter away and smiled up at the prince. "It's wonderful to meet you Prince Manfred." She attempted a curtsy – a southern custom Lady Summer had taught her about – but her shoe caught on the end of a knobbly turnip and she tripped and fell to the ground.

"Please, call me Prince Turnip," the prince said, as he watched the Britt daughters help their mother up. "A pleasure to make your acquaintances, ladies."

The prince jumped off his horse and shook their hands one by one. His fingers felt like a bucket of slippery eels. Then, he looked them up and down like a merchant appraising a barrel of whale oil. "Yes," he said with a purr. "They will do nicely."

"*They*?" the captain's wife said.

"Yes. I would very much like to marry them all."

"But, Mother," her daughters moaned. They pulled their greedy eyes away from the glittering gold chains and tugged on their mother's dress. "We don't want to share."

"Hush now, girls," the captain's wife hissed. She knew that a mother was meant to think the world of her daughters, but she also had to be realistic. She had now seen the type of ladies who lived in the South and, though it pained her to admit it, her own daughters' prospects were not the greatest. This would most likely be the best, perhaps the only, offer of marriage they received. But she did have one final question before she gave her six favourite daughters away.

"Just how rich are you, exactly?"

While Missus Britt mulled over Prince Turnip's marriage proposal in the South, Freydis Spits searched Nordlor's shore for a shell. The money

from her winter prediction had run out and she needed to find a new one to sell.

Freydis was about to stop searching for the day when a shell washed right up at her feet. She picked it up and raised it to her ear.

Words tumbled inside the shell so quickly that Freydis could not hear. She knew the fortune it held must be important, for she'd never heard a shell speak as urgently as this. But before Freydis could unjumble the words, a crab crawled out from the shell and bit her on the ear.

"Foxes and thunder!" Freydis screamed. She threw the shell on to the shore. It cracked and twenty words fluttered away on the wind. Freydis yanked on the crab until it released her ear. She knelt beside the broken shell and tried to piece it back together. But the shell was broken beyond repair, and the future inside was lost.

"Bears and wolves and thieves in the night!" Freydis cursed. She had really wanted to hear that fortune. She bet it would have been grand. After all, before it broke she had heard all sorts of glorious words: knife and death; betrayal and loss; and Oona and nardoo.

OONA'S BIRTHDAY SURPRISE

Two nights after the *Plucky Leopard* entered the Icelands, the first twinkling of Northern Lights appeared above the ship. With each passing night, the lights grew bigger and brighter until half the time you couldn't even see the stars for all the dazzling lights in front of them. To Oona, it felt like a present from the heavens: like the Lords and Ladies of the Sea were thanking her for saving Olf's life.

As they ploughed deeper into the Icelands, shards of ice built up around the ship. Haroyld warned Oona that if they put down anchor the sea

159

would freeze around them, and they wouldn't be able to move for half a year.

One night, as they looked up at the sky, Haroyld said, "The Northern Lights are so bright tonight: the brightest I've ever seen. I think they're shining for you, Oona. Happy birthday."

"It's my birthday?" Oona said. They had been at sea for so long she had lost track of time. Her father must have lost track of time too. He hadn't wished her a happy birthday all day, not even when she'd shown him all the fish she had caught for breakfast.

The navigator nodded. "Mathilde and I never forget the date."

Haroyld reached into his coat and pulled out a small gift. It was wrapped in brown paper and tied together with sailor's string.

Oona's eyes widened with surprise.

"It was you," she said. "You left all of those presents outside my bedroom window. But why?"

"Mathilde and I saw the way your family treated you and we didn't think it was right. Everyone deserves to feel special, to feel loved, to get a present on their birthday."

Though Oona was delighted to find out the identity of her secret friend, she was also slightly disappointed.

"What's wrong?" Haroyld asked when he saw this second feeling cross her face.

"It's nothing," Oona said. "Well..." Oona wanted to say something to Haroyld that she'd never felt brave enough to say to anyone before. But she was afraid she might hurt his feelings. "It's just, I thought someone younger might have given it to me. I thought maybe I might have had a secret friend my own age – a boy or a girl in Nordlor who actually liked me. None of them ever have, and I doubt any of them ever will. Except maybe for Trine."

"You're a rare girl, Oona," Haroyld said. "You're different to everyone else. But that's not a bad thing. Not at all. True, it does mean it will take you longer to find friends. But they are out there. And I bet that once you find them they will last a lifetime. Now, go on." Haroyld nodded to the present Oona still held. "Open it. I think it's the best one I've given you."

Being careful not to tear the paper, Oona unwrapped the gift: the only gift she would receive on this, her eleventh birthday. Inside lay a thick piece of parchment folded five times over. She unfolded the parchment and laid it on the deck. It was a map.

"I drew it myself," the navigator said. "I've marked all the places you have been, and you can fill in all the places you will go."

Unlike Haroyld's map that showed the Northern Sea, Oona's map had spaces that branched far beyond.

"It's so big," she said.

"That, Oona Britt, is because I have a feeling you are going to go very far."

Oona knelt to study the map more closely. She was admiring the detail when a loud *thud* sounded from the front of the ship. The world seemed to spin beneath her feet, like the ship was caught in the midst of a swirling current. But when Oona suggested this to Haroyld, the navigator shook his head.

"This isn't the feeling of being tossed about by the sea," Haroyld said. "This is what it feels like to stand on land *after* being at sea." Haroyld's face creased with confusion and then jumped with delight. "We've run aground, Oona," he said. "We've run aground in the middle of the sea. I think we've discovered a new island." And then, the navigator raced below deck so he could draw the island on his map.

HAROYLD'S ISLAND

By the time Haroyld returned with his map, half of the crew had come up on deck to see what had stopped the ship. They all, very quickly, came to the same conclusion.

"We've run aground on Fisherman's Hell!" they screeched into the night. "They're never going to let us off. No man ever leaves – remember Hans Pilfer?"

"Calm down," Haroyld said as he laid his map out on the deck. "We're fifty nautical miles north of Fisherman's Hell. This, men, is something else. Something new. A place that has never been mapped before."

Haroyld pulled a jar of ink and a quill from his pocket. With the ship still, it was easy to mark the spot where they currently were. But he had a problem. He did not know what to call the island.

"How about you call it Haroyld's Island?" Oona suggested.

The navigator blushed. "Oh, I don't think I could do that. Islands have only been named after captains, not navigators."

"Well, that's what I'm going to call it on mine," Oona said. And then, before Haroyld could protest, she borrowed his quill, dipped it in the ink and wrote "Haroyld's Island" just north of where Fisherman's Hell was marked on her own map.

By the time the ink dried all the crew, including the captain and Barnacles, had reached the deck and were looking out at the island in wonder.

"Never heard of an island this far north," one of them said.

"Surely it's been found before," said another. "Islands don't just pop up out of nowhere."

Curious to know more about this island, several of the men fetched lanterns from below deck. They attached them to fishing poles and hung them over the edge of the ship. In the flickering pools of orange light, a rocky shore appeared below.

"Well, there's only one thing for it," Oona's father said. "Let's explore."

Barnacles watched the crew leave the ship. He had sailed these waters for two hundred years and couldn't remember seeing an island here. It wasn't natural. It wasn't right. Yes, this island was very wrong, and he didn't want anything further to do with it. So, while all the men and the girl walked further away, Barnacles the cat turned around and darted below deck.

Haroyld's Island was not as big as Oona had hoped. Within one hour of walking they had reached the other side. It wasn't very exciting either. The same rocky shore they had sighted from the ship covered the entire surface. There were no trees, plants or grass. No living creatures, big or small. There were just rocks everywhere and you couldn't even pick them up. Oona had tried, but they appeared to be glued to the island itself.

"I might have to make the mark on my map a bit smaller," Haroyld said as they walked back towards the ship. Even though they now stood on land, he still led the way. "The island probably isn't even here in summer, not when the icebergs melt."

The crew crossed the island quickly. But when they reached the other side, there was a problem.

"The *Plucky Leopard*," Oona said. "It's gone."

When his ship first began to move, Barnacles thought nothing of it; the men had returned and they were sailing north once more. But as the hours passed, and he drifted in and out of sleep, he noticed something strange. The ship – his ship – was very, very quiet.

Barnacles left the navigator's cabin and walked into the men's quarters. All the bunks were empty. The mess hall was empty as well, so too the galley. He even checked in the storeroom, but no one was there.

Barnacles was about to search the deck when his eyes caught sight of something strange on the other side of the storeroom porthole. Instead of seeing the ocean and the bright Northern Lights, all he saw was a thick, green slimy tentacle. The men weren't moving the ship. A monster was.

"Face it," one of the men said as they circled the island for a third time. "You've lost your touch, old man."

"It's not that I can't navigate us back to the ship,"

Haroyld said. "It's that the ship, I'm afraid, is no longer here."

"What do you mean 'no longer here'?" This time the captain spoke. "We ran aground. We put down anchor. It can't exactly go anywhere without us."

"But it must have," Haroyld said. "We've walked around the edge of this island three times and the *Plucky Leopard* isn't here."

"It has to be here," said another of the men. "You just can't find it."

The men started to bicker amongst themselves. They were still arguing when the sun began to rise. The first light of day broke over the horizon. At first the light was thin and dim, and you could see nothing by it. But then, as it grew stronger, a shape appeared further down the shore.

"Look," Oona said. She pointed towards the shape she had just sighted. "You're all wrong. It's still here. *There's* the *Plucky Leopard*."

No longer run aground, the *Plucky Leopard* bobbed gaily in the waves. It wasn't very far from shore. But the sea was so cold and icy that if they tried to swim they would freeze before they reached it.

"Good spotting, Oona," her father said. He gave her an approving nod before his brow creased. "But how did it get out there?" He paused for a moment

and his brow creased even further. "It's that darn cat," he said. "I bet he's behind this. He's been after my ship for decades."

"His eyes have always looked shifty to me," one of the men agreed.

"Aye," said another. "My gran always told me never to trust cats. Hated cats, she did."

"It's not Barnacles," Oona said. "Look. Look what's sticking out of the water."

The crew walked closer to the water. As their vision sharpened, they saw several giant green tentacles reaching out of the sea and wrapping their suckers around the hull. For the first time that morning they could all agree on something.

"It's a monster!" they shrieked.

"Kill it!" they screamed.

One by one the men threw their flaming lanterns at the creature. As the small, oily flames soared over the sea, Oona noticed something. Eight tentacles grasped at the ship. If they punctured the wood, they would leave eight identical round holes in the hull. With a sinking feeling, Oona realized that this beast, or one very much like it, had destroyed the *Gandering Gull*.

At the same time Oona realized this, she also realized something else.

169

Fifty years ago, on their own journey north, the members of the *Gandering Gull* must have stumbled upon this beast. When its tentacles wrapped around their ship, they had used flames against it. But instead of burning the creature, they had accidentally burned their own ship. Now, the same was about to happen again.

"Stop," she yelled. "Stop!" she screamed at the men. "You're going to hit the ship. You're going to burn the *Plucky Leopard*."

"What else can we do?" Oona's father asked.

By now, six tentacles wrapped around the hull of his ship and another two twisted themselves up the masts. The creature held on so tightly that the wood beneath its suckers buckled. If they didn't do something, the *Plucky Leopard* would be lost even without the help of fire.

Oona was about to say she didn't know what they could do when she noticed something in the water. Just off the shore, a dark, green and slimy tentacle slithered beneath the waves. Oona followed the path it made. It led from Haroyld's Island all the way to the *Plucky Leopard*. A sick feeling washed over her. They weren't standing on an island. They were standing on the monster.

THE NORTHERN WING

Prince Turnip had not lied when he told the captain's wife that he was the richest man in the South. Along with possessing one thousand fields of turnips, he also owned the largest castle.

"Mother," Ina said when she saw the castle for the first time. "It's bigger than our house."

"It's bigger than all the houses on Whalebone Lane," Berit corrected.

"It's bigger than Nordlor itself," Sissel said.

"And soon it will all be yours," Prince Turnip said to his six future wives. "You can each have your own turret. You can stay there until the wedding."

There was only one negative that the Britt sisters could find. The whole place smelled of turnips, and within a day of arriving they smelled like turnips too. Still, it was a small price to pay for becoming princesses.

"Now—" the prince said. It was time to give his future wives a tour of his castle. He didn't want them getting lost or falling in the moat. "The kitchen is in the southern wing, along with the bakehouse and the Great Hall. I have five chefs skilled in making all the great dishes, like turnip mash, turnip soup and turnip pie. They work all through the day and night, so you can eat whenever you want."

While the Britts loved the idea of being able to eat on demand, they weren't too thrilled about the options available.

"Don't you eat anything that *doesn't* have turnips in it?" Trine asked hopefully.

The prince thought for a moment and then shook his head. "No. Now, let's move on to the western wing."

The prince led them across a large grass courtyard that separated the four stone wings of his castle. "Here you will find the chapel and the priest's house. He's the one who will marry us." He winked at his future wives before turning from the western wing and pointing up at the eastern one. "In there you will find the stables and my quarters. I also have a whole room just for counting my money. I do it every morning at dawn. I have so much that the counting takes me right through until lunch."

All the Britt sisters looked very impressed by this, but not as impressed as their mother. Since arriving at the castle, she had not stopped smiling and chuckling. Sometimes, if one of her daughters turned their head quick enough, they would catch her rubbing her hands together and whispering, "Money. Money. Money."

"And what do you do after that?" Sissel asked the prince. "What do you do after you have counted our— I mean, *your* money?"

"Why, I have lunch in the southern wing, and then I go to the northern one."

"Ooh," Onka said. "What's in the northern wing?"

"Now that, my dear Plonka," the prince said secretly, "is my favourite wing of all. But, alas, I cannot tell you what is in there. For, it is a surprise. A surprise that I will reveal to you all on our wedding day."

*

At the same moment her sisters were touring their future castle, Oona and the men of the *Plucky Leopard* remained trapped on Haroyld's Island. What had appeared to be her best birthday in eleven years had quickly turned into Oona's worst. As soon as she realized the truth about the island and the monster – the truth that they were one and the same – the creature had begun to move. Now the entire island was twisting and shaking in the water.

"What's happening?" the men cried. By now the trembling island had risen out of the ocean, and it felt like they were floating in the sky instead of in the sea.

"It's the creature," Oona said. "The creature *is* the island, and I think it's trying to throw us into the water."

As soon as Oona finished her sentence the creature got its wish. One of the men standing closest to the water's edge lost his footing and fell into the sea.

"Help!" the man screamed when his head emerged above the surface. "Help me. Quick!"

Two men standing close to the water gingerly reached out for their friend. But before their hands closed around his, something pulled him under. A few bubbles appeared on the surface, and then the water grew still.

Seconds passed. The island stopped moving. Oona looked towards their ship. Only seven tentacles remained wrapped around the *Plucky Leopard*. One was missing. A whole minute went by and then another. The fallen man did not resurface.

The crew's terror grew. They edged towards the centre of the island and huddled together. The eighth tentacle reappeared near the stern of their ship, and, once again, the island began to move. Only this time, instead of moving up, the island started to sink down.

The ocean grew nearer. The island grew smaller. Soon there would be no island left to stand on and they would all, like the first man, fall into the sea. With eight tentacles it wouldn't take long for the creature to grab and devour the entire crew.

Oona thought her life was over – she was going to die one day after turning eleven – but then she had an idea. While it may have been hard to hit the tentacles with their lanterns, it would not be so hard to hit the island itself.

"Put your lanterns on its back," Oona said. When none of the men listened, she grabbed her father's arm and shook it. "Father," she said, "they have to put the lanterns on the island. They have to push them into its back."

Oona's father was about to tell her to be quiet – a very common response he had voiced while they lived in Nordlor – but then he realized his daughter was right.

"Men?" he yelled. "Stop!" he screamed. "Press your lanterns into the monster's back."

When the words came from their captain, the men did as they were told. Instead of hurling the flames across the water they pressed them into the ground beneath their feet.

The flames leached out of the lanterns and licked at the rocks below. At first, nothing happened. But then, as the flames grew larger, the rocks melted and green, slimy skin appeared beneath. The island started to wriggle and then roll beneath their feet. A few of the men fell over and almost tumbled into the approaching sea.

Oona feared she had made a mistake; she had just angered the creature, not hurt it. But then a cry sounded from beneath the waves. The creature released the *Plucky Leopard* from its clutches and its tentacles raced back to the island, where the crew huddled on its back. Oona and the men had to duck and weave as the creature slammed its tentacles down on to its own body. But instead of extinguishing the flames, the tentacles fuelled them, and soon they were on fire too.

"We're going to die!" the men screamed as eight ribbons of giant fire danced around them. "We're going to burn!"

Oona feared they were right – this was the end – but then the sails on the *Plucky Leopard* rose into the air and billowed in the wind. The ship turned and began to move closer. Oona wondered which man was coming to save them. She looked around and counted all the crew. She realized the only person who could be on board wasn't a person at all. It was a cat.

Barnacles had not wanted to save the crew; he had wanted to turn around and sail far, far away. He may have loved adventures on the sea, but he did not love things like this: things that could get him killed. But just as he was about to turn the wheel away from the captain and his crew, Barnacles remembered something.

The memory was from two lifetimes ago. He rarely remembered moments that old. As soon as it came to him, he wished he could forget it.

Barnacles had been playing the fiddle for hours.

Yet still the men of the *Gandering Gull* kept cheering and calling out, "Encore! Encore!" The dining hall was ablaze with flames – lanterns burned in every corner to keep away the winter cold. Barnacles had just begun to play "The Northern Jig" when the ship ran aground.

Unlike Captain Britt, Captain Holm had not wanted to leave his ship.

"It's unnatural, men," he warned them when they ran up on to the deck. "I'd rather step on to Fisherman's Hell than this unknown place."

The older crew members listened – they had sailed these seas for two decades and trusted the captain with their lives – but some of the younger men did not. They started to whisper amongst themselves, whisper about finding hidden treasure, and against the captain's command they jumped off the ship and went to explore.

The men were gone for several hours. Captain Holm could have left, but instead he stayed and waited for them to return.

It was nearing dawn when the ship started to move. The captain yelled, "Put down anchor." But the anchor was already down.

Panic began to spread amongst the men. None knew what was happening. Their panic only grew

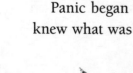

when sunlight broke and they saw the tentacles that held them.

Captain Holm ordered the masts to be raised and turned the wheel away from the island. But it was no use. The tentacles that held them refused to let go.

It was one of the fishermen – a man named Dag – who had the idea.

"We'll burn the creature. Then it'll let us go." He grabbed one of the lanterns from the dining hall and pressed the flame against a green tentacle. The monster hissed in pain and pulled back.

The rest of the men copied the first. They grabbed lanterns and held them against the tentacles. One by one the tentacles dropped away until there were only two left.

"That's the way, men," Captain Holm cried. "We'll be free of this monster yet!"

No sooner had the words left the captain's mouth when disaster struck. One of the men, eager to burn a tentacle wrapped around the forward mast, accidentally burned the mast instead. The white cloth exploded into red flames. Scraps of burning material fluttered down on to the deck. To Barnacles, it had looked like the entire sky was burning. When the cloth landed on the deck the wood caught alight.

The men tried everything to put out the flames. They doused them with seawater, smothered them with blankets and even tried to stomp the fire out with their feet. But it was no use. The flames kept burning. The whole ship went up. And, just after dawn, the forward mast snapped and fell on Barnacles' head.

Barnacles' hair rose up at the memory. He didn't want to die, not for a ninth and final time. And despite his negative feelings towards some of the crew, he didn't want them to die either. He could see only one path forward. The ship needed a crew to get it back to Nordlor safely, not just a cat. So, instead of turning the golden wheel away from the crew, he turned it towards them.

Barnacles scaled the masts. He spun the wheel. He moved faster than thirty men. He darted so quickly about the ship that he was just a ginger blur. By the time he reached the crew, the monster had sunk into the sea and they were treading water. Two men were helping to keep Olf afloat. Luckily, the flames which had engulfed the creature had also warmed the sea. The ice had melted, but it was still cold enough to kill them if they stayed in for long enough.

Barnacles lowered a whaleboat into the ocean.

The captain, as custom, climbed in first. He turned back to the men still treading water. Instead of reaching out for Haroyld or Peder or the flailing Olf, he held his hand towards his daughter.

"In you come, Oona," he said. "You deserve it." He reached out and, with his large, weathered hand, hauled her out of the sea.

"FORGET THE WHALE!"

Birds chirped in the green fields surrounding Turnip Castle. The day was bright and sunny, and the smell of southern blossoms hung heavy in the air.

"I bet Oona wishes she had come with us now," Sissel said. "She probably hasn't seen the sun in weeks."

"In months," Berit corrected.

"In a whole year," the twins proclaimed.

They were sitting down to breakfast in the Great Hall with their mother. Their future husband was absent: he was in the eastern wing counting all his money. But while the Britts may have been enjoying the weather they still weren't enjoying the food.

"This is the third day in a row we've had to eat cold turnip porridge for breakfast," Ina said as she used her spoon to push the grey lumps around her bowl.

"And it's not going to get any better," Onka wailed. "One of the cooks said we're having turnip salad for lunch."

Only one of the Britt sisters didn't complain about the food. Two days earlier, while she was walking around the castle grounds, Trine had met a boy her own age called Hermann who also hated turnips. Hermann was an apprentice gardener and in his spare time, when he wasn't tending to the turnips, he was secretly growing his own patch of carrots and swedes. He had been sharing these with Trine every day before lunch. Trine hadn't told her sisters about this secret garden. They ate so much that all the carrots and swedes would be gone in a day.

To keep their minds off the terrible food, the older Britt sisters started to talk about the mysterious northern wing. Since seeing the outside of it three days before they hadn't stopped talking about what could be hidden inside. Each sister had their own theory.

"I bet it's full of treasure," Sissel said. "After all, every castle has a treasure room, and the prince didn't mention one of those during the tour."

"I think it's a swimming pool," Berit said. "I've heard they're very popular in the South."

"Me too," Ina agreed.

"I bet it just holds more turnips," the twins said mournfully as they shovelled more cold porridge into their mouths.

"It can't be that," Trine said. "If it held turnips we'd be able to smell them leeching through the walls."

"Well, if you're so smart," Plonka said, "what do you think is inside?"

Trine paused for a moment before she answered. Along with sharing carrots and swedes, Hermann had shared with her a little bit about the northern wing. He hadn't said much, for fear he would get in trouble, but he had said enough to make Trine worry. Hermann had said that he didn't want a nice person like Trine to end up inside the northern wing. When Trine had asked him why, Hermann had refused to answer.

"I'm not sure," Trine finally said. She knew that if she mentioned Hermann or his warning, her sisters would tell everyone. And Hermann had been so nice to her, she didn't want to get him in trouble. "I just have a feeling that something bad might be inside."

"Don't be silly, Trine," their mother said. "Why would the prince keep something bad inside his castle? I bet Sissel's right. I bet it's full of treasure."

"See," Sissel said with a smug smile.

"But how can you know for sure?" Trine asked.

"I have a sense for these things," Sissel said. "And," she added a few seconds later, "I heard one of the maids speaking about it."

Everyone at the table stopped eating and looked towards Sissel. "What did she say?" they all said at once.

"She said that the northern wing is full of priceless treasures that Prince Turnip and his family have been collecting for almost one hundred years. And I bet he's not letting us see it until the wedding because it's going to be our wedding gift. He's going to split all the treasure between the six of us. We're not just going to be princesses. We're going to be the richest princesses in all of the South."

While her sisters' faces lit up with greed, Trine's remained creased with worry. Even though she had known Hermann for only two days, she trusted him more than her sisters. There was something nice about him. Something sweet about him. In a way, he reminded her of Oona. She had a feeling that out of everyone in Turnip Castle – out of all the maids and cooks and the prince himself – Hermann was the only one telling her the truth.

Oona leant over the side of the crow's nest and looked down at the ship below. Little pools of flickering light lit the deck. The day after they escaped the island creature, the darkness of true winter had hit. The sun stopped rising in the morning, and every day and night grew black. To mark dawn a bell now tolled below deck, and lanterns and stars became the only source of light. Oona pulled her eyes away from the ship and looked south.

A week had passed since they escaped the island creature. No one knew for sure if it had died from the flames or if it had only been injured. In case it was the latter and the wicked creature came after them, they were taking turns keeping watch.

From where she stood in the crow's nest, Oona felt like the queen of the world. She imagined that if she looked hard enough she could see all the way back to Nordlor and perhaps even further beyond. If she had a telescope she might have even been able to see the South. She wondered what her sisters were doing and if Trine was happy down there. She hoped, very much, that she was.

Oona was nearing the end of her shift when she spotted something in the darkness beside the ship. A creature was swimming beneath the waves. Her heart skipped a beat and she went to scream the alarm. But then she realized something that made her heart race even faster.

The creature swimming alongside the ship wasn't like the one they had just escaped. Instead of murky green – the kind of colour that sucked all other colours in – this creature was shimmering, glistening, twinkling beneath the water, like it was making light instead of taking it away.

As soon as Oona's eyes fell upon the brightness, she knew what the creature was. She slid down the mast – even faster than Barnacles – and raced below deck to get Haroyld.

"Look," Oona said, leaning over the side of the ship. The navigator stood beside her. "It's a nardoo."

Oona pointed towards the water. A giant creature – four times the length of their ship and at least twice as wide – crashed through the waves.

Thousands of scales lined its back. They twinkled and shimmered like ribbons of smoke and twine in the dark.

"I think you're right," Haroyld said. "It's wonderful."

"Magical," Oona replied. "Even more magical than I ever imagined."

Oona was helping Haroyld up on to the rail when she heard a voice behind them.

"Magical?" a man said. "What's magical?" He walked past them and stared into the water. "What in the sea is that?" he cried.

"It's a nardoo," Oona said.

"A nardoo?" The man smirked. He looked ready to mock her for believing in a children's tale, but then a different thought came upon him. He turned from the sea and ran across the deck. A minute later, all the men of the *Plucky Leopard* raced over.

"This better be good," they mumbled.

The man who first saw the nardoo led the others toward the starboard side. The *Plucky Leopard* keeled to the right as they leant over the rail and peered down into the water.

"Would you look at that?" one of the men said.

"Why I never," said another.

"What's all this commotion?" yelled a third. It was Oona's father. He had been downstairs in his cabin when the ship veered to the side. He had raced up to see what had caused it. "Have we hit an iceberg?"

"It's not that, Captain," said one of the men. "Oona spotted something in the water."

The captain's eyes jumped with delight. He turned to his daughter and asked, "Is it a whale?"

Oona shook her head. "It's even better."

Curious to see what could be better than a whale, Oona's father crossed the deck and peered over the side of his ship. A silence fell amongst the men while the captain studied the ocean below. It was finally broken when Oona's father turned around, smiled in the midday darkness and said, "Forget the whale, boys. We've got something bigger to catch!"

THE HUNT

At the captain's order, the *Plucky Leopard* took chase. The ship moved slowly through the water at first, and it looked like the nardoo would escape. But then the wind picked up and billowed the sails. The *Plucky Leopard* surged through the sea, like it was a creature of the ocean itself, adorned with fins and a tail of its own.

As they hunted the nardoo across the water, the men on board took turns telling tales about the creature. Only their tales were not at all like the one Oona had read in her birthday book.

"The nardoos did not make the North. They

destroyed it," one of the men said as he tightened the forward mast. "They ate all the fish in the sea, tore apart all of the ships and killed all of the men inside."

"Some say that's what sunk the *Wandering Walrus*," said another. "It chased the ship for weeks and then, finally, it closed in and ripped the great whaler apart."

"I heard that its heart is made of gold," whispered another. "Just one nardoo heart could make all of us rich."

"They say," said another, "that whoever kills a nardoo will have good luck for seventy years. And if you drink its blood you will gain the strength of one thousand men."

"That's not true," Oona said to the men. "The nardoos aren't like that at all. They're good and they're kind and they make the North the North."

The men around Oona laughed. Only Haroyld agreed with her.

"Right you are, Oona," he said sadly. "Right you are."

It was when Oona heard the tone of Haroyld's voice that she knew for certain what her father planned to do. She had come north to see a nardoo, but her father wanted to kill it.

192

"I think we should leave it alone," Oona said. "I think we should let it go."

The men around her laughed again. They turned their backs and continued to move the ship forward.

Even with the wind on their side it took a long time for the *Plucky Leopard* to close in on the nardoo. Several hours passed before the ship grew close enough to launch the whaleboats. Oona was boarding the fourth whaleboat with Haroyld when her father called her towards the first.

"Tonight you sit with me," he said. A lantern from the deck had been tied to the front of the whaleboat so they could see the way ahead. The other four boats shimmered in the light cast from their own flames.

Oona followed her father into the first whaleboat. When she stepped inside she saw a large net and a giant harpoon. A sense of dread settled over her.

With the weight of seven people weighing it down, the whaleboat did not rock as it was lowered into the sea.

"Row! Row! Row!" Oona's father yelled when the boat touched the waves. "Row hard to port!"

The first whaleboat moved out into the open sea.

Four others followed. The captain's eyes grew wild and crazy, like a fox on the hunt. Excitement made his mouth foam like the sea before a storm. Oona did not look like her father at all. She looked scared and lonely and sad.

"Father?" Oona said as they rowed deeper into the night. She tugged on the coat of his jacket until he turned around.

"What is it, Oona?" he said.

At first, Oona didn't say anything; her words got caught in her throat. She knew her father would not like what she had to say, but she also knew she would not like herself if she didn't say it. Eventually, she swallowed her fear and said, "Please don't, Father. Please don't do it. Let the nardoo live."

As the words left her mouth Oona felt a glimmer of hope. She knew her father never would have listened to her in the past, but perhaps now, after all the time they had spent together, he would.

But she was wrong. The captain pushed her hand away, told her to keep quiet and turned back to face the murky night.

The five whaleboats moved swiftly west. The light of their lanterns did little to pierce the night that loomed dark around them. But then, other lights appeared up ahead. Beneath the waves, the nardoo's scales glistened. The light they cast – gold, silver and purple – stretched from the creature's back and up into the sky. The lights rose higher and higher until they looked like they brushed against the moon itself. As she tilted her head back to watch, Oona gasped. The nardoos did not swim beneath the Northern Lights. They made them.

The closer the whaleboats got to the creature the brighter the lights in the sky became. Soon, night appeared as bright as day. In the newly made light a white mountain appeared.

"What's that?" Oona said. Despite the brightness in the sky, the air remained cold. When she spoke, her breath left her mouth as ice and fell with a rattle beside her feet.

"An iceberg," her father whispered.

Oona had expected her father to be worried: sailors hated icebergs. But his eyes widened with excitement, not fear.

"Go round!" Oona's father yelled towards the boats. "Go wide!" he screamed. "We'll block it off. Trap it! Remove all chances of escape!"

The whaleboats spread out around the nardoo. Soon, the creature loomed before them.

"Quiet now," the captain whispered. "We do not want to gally the beast."

The men stopped rowing. A silence filled the air. Then, a gentle humming sounded from beneath the water. It made the surface of the sea ripple. The sound made Oona feel old and young: like she had lived for one million years and would live for one million more. It made her feel like she was at home even though she was one thousand miles out to sea. But most of all, it made her feel frightened of what the men around her were about to do.

Slowly, with their oars only just brushing the water, the boats closed in. The captain picked up the harpoon and raised it to his shoulder. Then, before Oona could cry out for him to stop, he fired into the night. The harpoon sailed through the air and landed with a splash in the water. Oona's father had missed.

The captain hauled the harpoon back in. He was preparing to launch it for a second time when his target moved.

The nardoo reared up out of the water. It rose higher and higher until it looked even larger than the iceberg looming behind it. The creature paused for a moment. The lights in the sky stilled. And then, slowly at first but then very fast, it fell back down.

The nardoo landed on the water with a monstrous slap. The ocean rose up around it, and a wave higher than the *Plucky Leopard* raced towards them.

All the crew, including Oona, stared in horror as the wave rolled closer. It was so large and so black that it blocked out the stars and then the moon and then the Northern Lights. Soon, all they could see was the flickering of five small lanterns and all they could hear was water roaring towards them. Then, the lanterns went out with a silent hiss, and they were engulfed by the wave.

The force of the wave pushed the whaleboats beneath the ocean. Water flooded inside. Oona felt the boat tip. She grabbed hold of the edge and held on as tightly as she could. Just as the boat was about to flip and sink slowly to the ocean floor, the wave that had swallowed them up let them go.

Almost like the creature had called its name, the water surged back to the nardoo. The whaleboats rose to the surface. The lanterns were lost, but none of the crew.

"That was close," said the man sitting beside Oona. It was Peder: the man whose son went to school with her. Peder's hair and beard were caked in ice and his knuckles were white.

The rest of the men laughed. Though they all smiled, they looked nervous.

"I think we should head back," Oona said.

This time, none of the men argued. But her father did.

"Don't be a coward, Oona," he said. "We can't go back now. Not when we've almost caught it."

The captain had only just finished speaking when the nardoo reared up again. It flipped in the air – like it was doing a trick – and fell back down. A second wave, even larger and faster than the first, careered into the five whaleboats.

This time the whaleboats were dragged right down into the sea. If any of the crew had been brave enough to open their eyes they would have seen creatures swimming beside them that lived so deep in the water they had never seen the sky.

The nardoo took longer to call the second wave back. Some of the crew could not hold their breath for that long. They exhaled one final mouthful of air and then breathed in water. As the sea filled their lungs, they sunk to a place so deep and dark that no living creature called it home.

When the wave finally receded, and the

whaleboats rose back to the surface, only four boats out of five remained. The third boat – and all the men inside – was gone. One of the men in Oona's boat had also been claimed by the sea. It was Peder. Oona imagined his son all the way back in Nordlor. Perhaps he was answering a question in class or maybe he was sitting down to dinner with his mother. Wherever he was, he had no idea he had just lost his father.

Oona's mind was dragged back to the Icelands when her own father, still living, rose to his feet once more. Despite the ferocity of the sea, the captain had not lost his grip on the harpoon. Before the nardoo could claim any more of his men, he aimed the weapon and fired into the night. This time he did not miss. The harpoon speared the nardoo in the centre of its back.

A monstrous cry shook the air. The whaleboats rattled and their wood splintered. Around them, the sea screamed and the sky cried. The lights in the heavens trickled down, fading as they fell, until all the rainbow lights went out. After twelve hours on the hunt, and the loss of six men, the crew of the *Plucky Leopard* had caught the nardoo.

OONA'S CHANCE

A deadly silence fell over the sea. Oona had never heard a quietness so loud. The wind had stopped. The waves had stopped. It felt like time itself had stopped. Then, Oona's father yelled, "Grab the net. Let's trap this beast!"

The men rowed towards one another. Two men from each boat grabbed a corner of the giant net. Then, they spread back out. At the captain's command, they sent the net flying through the air. It landed with a heavy *thud* across the nardoo's back. The men hauled the injured creature in.

By now, the nardoo had sunk low into the water,

but some of its back remained above the sea. Its scales glistened softly in the night, but they weren't as bright as they used to be. Oona wondered if the creature was dying.

The men dragged the nardoo closer until it brushed against the side of the first whaleboat. The scales on its back were smooth and looked like ancient stone. Oona's breath caught in her throat and her skin tingled.

"Oona," the captain said.

"Yes?" Oona looked up towards her father. She had been sitting, frozen, beside him ever since the harpoon was fired. She saw something glistening in his hand. It was his whalebone knife.

"My grandfather carved this from the bone of the first whale he ever killed. Then, he handed it down to his son who handed it down to me. I always wanted a son to pass it down to. But now, Oona." He father looked into her eyes. They were the same shade of blue as her own. "I would like you to have it."

"Me?" Oona said.

The captain nodded. He held the blade out towards his daughter.

"Yes. It's your knife now."

With shaking hands, Oona reached out and

took the blade from her father. The knife felt heavy in her hands, and she wondered if she would ever have the strength to wield it.

"Now," the captain said, nodding towards the nardoo. "Up you get."

"What?" Oona asked.

"This is your chance, Oona. This is your chance to show me what you can do."

Oona's eyes widened with horror. It was bad enough that the men were going to kill the nardoo. She didn't want to do it herself.

"Don't worry yourself, girl," her father growled. "You can't kill the thing with that." He nodded towards the knife. "I just want you to make the first cut."

When Oona's father saw that his daughter was about to argue, he said sternly, "It's a great honour to deliver the first cut, Oona, even just to a whale. But this is no whale. This is a nardoo. A creature of legend. No man has ever captured one of them."

Fear of upsetting her father made Oona stand up. With shaking legs, she made her way towards the side of the boat.

"You'll have to lean right out," her father instructed.

Oona leant over the side of the boat until her

arms were directly above the creature's back. The nardoo rocked against the small boat and icy water splashed across Oona's fingers.

"That's my girl," her father said. "Push it right through the skin."

With a final glance at her father, to make sure she was doing it right, Oona drew back the whalebone knife and then drove it forward. But instead of cutting through the nardoo's flesh, Oona cut through a piece of the rope that held it down.

"Never mind," her father said. It had looked, to him, like her grip had slipped. "You'll get it the second ti—"

Oona swung the knife for a second time. Another line of rope fell away, and then a third was slashed in half by the knife.

"What are you doing?" her father cried. When Oona cut a fourth line of rope he understood exactly what she was up to. His daughter was not trying to kill the nardoo; she was trying to save it. He went to snatch the knife away, but before he could Oona leapt free of the boat and landed on the nardoo's back.

The creature rose and fell in the waves beneath Oona's feet. A humming sound ran up through her legs. Despite the cold air and the icy water lapping against her shoes, Oona felt warm, like she was sitting beside a fire in Nordlor.

Ignoring the yells of the men, and her father's cries most of all, Oona knelt and cut through the rope. Slowly, piece by piece, the giant net slipped away.

"Go on!" the captain cried to his men. "What are you waiting for? Stop her. Stop her now!"

But fear of falling into the sea held the men of the *Plucky Leopard* back. Instead of stopping Oona, they watched from the safety of the whaleboats as she continued to cut the great creature free.

Soon, Oona had cut away every piece of the net except one. She placed the blade of her knife beneath it, and the rope snapped in two. The entire net slid into the water and was swallowed by the dark sea.

Oona had expected the nardoo to swim away, but it remained bobbing in place. For a moment, she feared it was dead – she was too late in her quest to save it – but then in the moonlight she caught a glimpse of one final piece of rope.

"Don't you do it," Oona's father yelled as she crept across the nardoo's back. The rope that held the harpoon stretched out of the creature's side and into her father's hands. "Don't you dare," her father screamed across the sea. "Oona," he yelled when she reached the harpoon, "If you do this, I'll never forgive you."

For a moment, Oona paused. She looked across the water to her father. She had wanted so much for him to love her and for a while she thought that he had. But now, standing in the middle of the Icelands on the back of a nardoo, she realized the truth.

For over ten years Oona's father had treated her badly. On the night she was born he left her alone in the Sinking Eel. For the first decade of her life he made her sleep in a cold, dark attic. And as she neared her eleventh birthday he had tried to send her far away to marry a stranger. He had only started to like her, to be proud of her, when she grew brave and bold enough to do things that helped him. By saving Olf, she had made sure her father kept having nice dinners every night at sea. By learning how to steer and fish, she had reduced the amount of work he had to do. And by killing the creature disguised as an island, she had saved his life and his ship. The moment she tried to do something that didn't suit him – the moment she tried to save the nardoo instead of killing it – he had returned to his old self.

Oona had been so busy wishing her father would like her, she hadn't stopped to realize that maybe she didn't like him. This realization made the choice before her easy. She turned from her father and cut the final piece of rope. It went limp in the captain's hands.

Oona looked down at the nardoo. The harpoon had left a large wound in its back. Something thick and black leaked out from the cut.

"You poor thing," Oona whispered. She placed her father's knife in the pocket of her coat and wrapped her hands around the end of the harpoon. "This is going to hurt," she said.

Oona took a deep breath and pulled on the harpoon. The piece of iron moved slightly in her fingers. The creature wailed and cried beneath her, and more black liquid trickled out into the sea.

"This is the last bit," Oona promised. "In a moment, you'll be free." She gave one final yank on the harpoon, and it slipped out of the creature's back. The force of the pull was so great that the harpoon flew right over the nardoo and landed with a splash in the sea.

Beneath Oona, the creature hummed with delight. A spout of rainbow shot into the air, and the sky above her head exploded with light. The water around the nardoo stirred as the creature's fins and tail moved once more with life. Waves reared up around it, and the nardoo began to swim away.

With no time to spare, Oona bounded and slid across the nardoo's gigantic back. She raced towards the boat that held her father. It was the only one close enough for her to reach. She could see him watching her draw near. When she reached the edge of the nardoo's back, she took a great leap into the air. As her legs floated above the icy sea, her father turned from her and said to his men, "Row."

With one movement of their arms, the gap between the whaleboat and the nardoo became too much. Instead of landing on wood, Oona fell through a sheet of ice and into the sea. She distinctly heard her father yell, "Keep rowing!" and then her head went under.

This far north the sea was so cold that it hurt when you hit it. As soon as Oona went under her lungs gasped for air, and when she opened her mouth icy shards of water flooded in. Oona kicked her feet towards the surface, but the water made her body slow. Her heart ached as it struggled to pump blood to her arms and legs. Oona was

slipping, flittering, between sleep and awake, between life and death, when she felt something push beneath her.

It's the nardoo, Oona thought. Just like she had saved it, the nardoo had come back to save her.

THE ICY RIVER

When Oona next awoke, she lay in a pool of ice on the deck of the *Plucky Leopard*. The four remaining whaleboats were lined up beside her. The rainbow lights in the sky had run away and now the heavens looked empty.

"The nardoo," Oona said. The crew stood in a circle, looking down at her. None of them looked happy. "The nardoo – it saved me."

"What are you blabbing on about, girl?" one of the men said. "The nardoo didn't save you. It swam away and left you to drown."

"But. . ." Oona couldn't understand. She had felt

the creature below her in the water. She had felt it push her to safety. So, if it hadn't been the creature who had saved her, who or what had?

"It was Haroyld." This time the captain spoke. "He was the one who saved you. The darn fool jumped in as we were rowing back. No idea why he did it."

"But it can't have been him." Oona searched the faces around her. The navigator was not there. "Where is he?"

"Below deck," her father said. "The sea has all but claimed him. I doubt he'll last the night."

The captain stepped forward and knelt beside his daughter. "Do you know what catching that nardoo would have done for me?" he growled. "I would have been famous North-wide. For hundreds of years men would have spoken my name. 'Captain Britt: the greatest fisherman who ever lived. While all the other men hunted whales, he hunted nardoos.' But not any more, Oona. You ruined it. You ruined everything." He reached into her wet pocket and took back his whalebone knife. "I gave you your chance," he said, "and you won't be getting another. From this day on, you are no longer my daughter." Then, he stood up, turned his back on his seventh daughter and went to steer his ship.

*

A few weeks ago, Oona would have been devastated if her father had said those things. But now she had something far more important to worry about.

Oona found Haroyld in his cabin. He was lying in bed. He looked like he was sleeping, only his skin was coloured blue. Barnacles was there too, curled up on the navigator's chest. The cat opened one eye when Oona entered. Then, he closed it very quickly.

Oona pulled a chair over to the bed and sat down. She took hold of Haroyld's hand. It felt as cold as the Northern Sea.

"It's not fair," she said as she looked down at the man who had jumped into the icy sea to save her. "This was your last trip. You were meant to make it back to Nordlor so you could retire and do all sorts of wonderful things. You were going to show me your maps too, remember?"

The navigator did not respond.

"It's all my fault," Oona said. "This trip was a mistake. I never should have come. I should have just gone south with my sisters. Then no one would have been hurt."

Again, the navigator did not move. As Oona looked down at him, a pool of sadness filled her

body. Haroyld was nothing like her father. When she had first sneaked on board, instead of taking her back to a life she hated he had fought to let her build a life she would love. When all the other men had been cruel to her, he had been kind. And when all the other men left her to drown in the sea, he had jumped in to save her. Even though the captain ranked first on the ship, to Oona, Haroyld ranked even higher.

While Oona looked at Haroyld she noticed something poking out from the pile of wet clothes beside his bed. She dropped to the ground and carefully pulled a piece of soggy parchment out of the navigator's coat. She tried to unfold the parchment, but it broke and fell to the floor. Haroyld's map – the map he had spent fifty years drawing – was ruined.

"I'm so sorry," Oona said.

Remembering her own map, Oona ran to the storeroom and retrieved it. Then, she returned to the navigator's cabin.

While Barnacles continued to sleep on the old man's chest, Oona found Haroyld's ink and quill and some folded parchment in a box. She laid the parchment across the floor and placed her map beside it. Then, very carefully, so the tilt of the ship did not ruin the marks, she started to draw him a new one.

Barnacles was disgusted. After the men hauled poor Haroyld out of the sea, they had shoved him into his cabin and left him there to die. It had been left up to Barnacles to change the navigator into a dry set of clothes and tuck him into bed. Then, he had lain on the man's chest to keep him warm.

Barnacles had not been able to sleep a wink since. Fear kept him awake: fear that the navigator would stop breathing and never rise to pat him again. He was still awake when the girl, Oona, came in. She sat beside the kind old man and spoke to him. When she found his spoiled map, she had started to draw him a new one. She was still there now, five hours on, trying to get the marks just right.

As Barnacles watched the girl work, a wave of guilt and then another of shame washed over him. It had been wrong to lock her in the storeroom all those weeks ago so Olf would get angry. It had been wrong to rip those eight holes in her coat. It had been wrong to chop off her hair. And it had been wrong to slip those old fish bones into the captain's soup so Oona would get in trouble and he would be praised as a hero.

214

By breaking the rules, Oona had saved the *Plucky Leopard*, not sunk it. If Oona hadn't stowed away, Olf the cook would have drowned. If Oona hadn't hidden on board, the crew would have been killed by the island creature. And if Oona hadn't run away to sea, a nardoo – one of the greatest creatures in the Northern Sea – would have died a horrible death.

For the first time since they left Nordlor, Barnacles saw the truth. The female child wasn't half bad. In fact, she might just be better than the entire crew put together. All of them except, of course, for Haroyld. And, if he could have his own way, there would only be two people on his crew list: the girl and the navigator. The other men could drown as far as he was concerned, especially the heartless captain.

Haroyld's wife woke with a jolt. Despite the still night air, the shutters on the bedroom window had blown open. Even though it was too dark to see her clock, Mathilde knew what time it was. The shutters always blew open, every morning, at two. She and Haroyld had even tried barricading the shutters with a thick iron lock, but no matter how large or strong the bolt, they would always break free and swing for hours in an unseen and unfelt wind.

For years Mathilde and Haroyld had wondered why this happened. Then, by chance, one evening in a harbour to the north, Haroyld met a survivor of the ship their cottage was hewn from. He recalled the night that the *Little Skipper* was lost. A great storm had lashed the boat for hours until finally, at two in the morning, the wind had ripped the bow right off.

Mathilde climbed out of bed and hurried over to the window. Despite wearing four coats and three pairs of mittens, the cold air still reached her. Freydis Spits may have been wrong about an early winter, but she had not been wrong about the deadliest, darkest and coldest winter in fifty years. It was like the sun had forgotten about Nordlor, perhaps about the North all together, and instead of rising bright above them every day it didn't rise above them at all. Almost a week had passed since she had seen the sun and sometimes she feared she would never see it again.

Everyone in Nordlor felt the same. Hardly anyone left their homes any more – except to fight over items at the weekly markets – and when they did they passed one another in silence and despair. Nordlor had become a village full of walking ghosts: a town inhabited by people paler than the moon and colder than the winter wind. It felt like every piece of the village was slowly dying in the darkness, and by the time the sun returned there would be nothing left.

Mathilde reached out and grasped the shutters. She held onto the wood as tight as her old hands would let her and pulled them closed. But the moment she let go, they swung back open. It used to be an annoyance, being woken by the shutters, but now it was a danger.

The cold of winter had made the villagers hungrier than usual, and they had eaten through most of their supplies. The elders had ordered more food be brought in from the surrounding towns and villages. But snowstorms, darkness and winds so strong they blew grown horses away stopped the supplies from reaching them.

Now, throughout Nordlor people were climbing into houses at night and stealing what little food was kept inside. Mister Bjorkman's tower had been robbed sixteen times. The thieves only stopped when there was no food – no whale meat or reindeer jerky – left to steal. In every lane, street and passage people were locking doors that had never been locked before and bolting windows that had, for over a century, been left open.

The village wasn't only running low on food. It was running low on light, blankets and clothes. It was even running low on wood. Things were getting so desperate that instead of being built back up into something new, the *Gandering Gull* had been ripped apart and shared amongst the villagers for firewood. The already burned wood had been burned again and now all that remained was ash. If the *Plucky Leopard* didn't return with supplies soon, it wouldn't just be thieves sneaking into houses at night. Death would slink inside too.

Unable to close the shutters, Mathilde looked beyond them instead. The lane outside was silent and still. Above the rooftops, she glimpsed the river that led north. She wondered how far away Haroyld was now and what he was doing. She imagined he was smoking his pipe somewhere – Arctic strawberry flavour – and looking up at the stars.

Mathilde was about to look up at the stars too, when her eyes caught sight of something in the water. A feeling of deep fear washed over her. Ice crystals had formed on the surface of the river. Soon, the water would freeze over and even Haroyld with his stars and maps would not be able to find a path back.

FREYDIS' FINAL PREDICTION

After Oona freed the nardoo it did not come back. The Northern sky grew even darker. Winter closed in. Blackness filled the air and the chunks of ice that loomed around the *Plucky Leopard* rose even higher than the nardoo itself.

"I doubt it even was a nardoo," one of the men muttered as they continued to plough a course north. "Probably just a deformed whale, like those elks born with two heads."

"And it didn't even fly," whined another. "I heard they're meant to fly."

"Well," said a third, "I would have preferred to

catch a deformed whale rather than no whale at all. Now everyone in the village will starve, and men will start eating each other in the streets. That's what happened in Islo when the *Bobbing Tarsk* failed to bring in a whale."

"Don't be so dramatic," Olf said. "We've caught enough fish to feed the village. Nordlor can survive one winter without a whale."

"Let's not talk about that yet," the captain snapped. He had taken a break from steering the ship and had come to hear what his men were talking about. "Not when we're still heading north." Besides, he thought to himself, this wasn't about feeding the village. This was about him. Imagine bringing back fish in lieu of a whale. The shame. The embarrassment. That might do for other captains – for lesser captains – but it wouldn't do for Captain Britt.

"About that, Captain," one of the men said cautiously. "When will we, um, be heading south?"

"Soon," the captain grumbled.

"How soon?" asked another of his men. "I don't want us to return without a whale, only, it's getting awfully dark up here."

"And cold," said another. "Cold even for the North."

"And the ice," Olf added. "It's getting awful big, Captain. Big enough to sink a ship."

The captain growled and stared at his men. He wanted to tell them off for being weak: gutless as a gutted fish. But, truth was, they were right. Winter settled upon them swiftly, and the further north they travelled the more dangerous the season became.

"All right," he said reluctantly. "We will sail on for three more days. If we don't spot a whale by then we will turn back to Nordlor. Captain's promise."

"The leopard seal leads us north," Oona whispered as she stared up at the sky. Barnacles was below deck with Haroyld. Six days had passed since the navigator dived into the sea to save her, and he had not awoken. Now, it was up to Oona to guide the ship forward.

"The bear shows us to the east," Oona said. It was three hours into the day, but the sky remained dark. "The owl shows us to the west." She looked up at the owl-shaped constellation twinkling in the dark day sky. "And if you follow the nardoo, why, it will take you all the way home."

Oona's voice cracked when she said the final

sentence: the same sentence Haroyld had said to her not long after she had been discovered on board. For the last three nights, the nardoo had been missing from the sky. While she had told the men that she knew what she was doing, secretly she had no idea. She may have had her own map, but she was not a navigator. Not a proper one. Only Haroyld was one of them, and if he didn't wake up Oona had a feeling the *Plucky Leopard* would never find its way home.

While Oona tried her best to guide the *Plucky Leopard* through the Icelands, her six sisters prepared for their wedding. Forget hand-me-downs from Lady Summer: Prince Turnip had paid for the finest seamstress in the South to make them each a custom wedding dress. He'd also organized for a shoemaker to craft six pairs of diamond-encrusted slippers for them to wear as they walked down the aisle. As the wedding neared, only one thing was missing.

"I so wish Father could be here," Ina said as she, her sisters and their mother completed the final dress fitting.

"I hope he's OK," Berit said. It had been four months since he waved them goodbye from the gates of Nordlor. A lot could have happened in that time.

"I'm sure he's fine," their mother said. "He'd have caught a whale by now. He's probably hauling it into the village as we speak."

Only one of the Britt sisters looked unhappy as she tried on her wedding dress. For weeks, Hermann had been warning Trine about the northern wing. Trine had also tried warning her mother and her sisters, but they had laughed her off and said she was being silly. Ina had even suggested she had sea-squelch for brains, just like their youngest sister.

Though Ina had meant this as an insult, Trine had taken it as inspiration. She had asked herself, "What would Oona do if she were in my shoes?" It hadn't taken long for Trine to work it out. Oona would say, "Forget the money! Forget the crown! Forget getting married!" Then, she would have kicked off the silly southern shoes and set out on an adventure of her own.

Trine wasn't bold enough or brave enough to do that. But she did feel bold and brave enough to set out on an adventure with someone else. And she knew just who that someone else might be.

*

Several hundred miles away, Freydis Spits stood in Nordlor's main square. Snow drifted down around her, and the wind worked itself into a gale. Three months had passed since she predicted winter would come early and now it was well and truly here. Even the sun had fled to escape it. Now, instead of bright light streaming down from the sky, fires fuelled by all sorts of items – cloth and wood and even seashells – burned around the main square.

Despite the weather and darkness, a large crowd had gathered for the weekly markets, not that there was much to buy. But Freydis wasn't there to go shopping. She was there to make an investment: an investment in her future. She had discovered a shell just that morning which held a grand prediction. And, if it turned out to be true, her reputation in the North would be restored. She would, once again, be able to charge for her fortunes. She would, once again, be rich!

"People of Nordlor!" Freydis cried from the centre of the village's main square. "And people from far beyond," she added with a dramatic flair and a wink to Lady Summer. "Gather around to hear a grave prediction. A prediction – I promise – that will not be proven wrong. Here, here," she whispered. "Come in closer," she hissed as the curious crowd moved in. "I have a very special fortune to tell. A free prediction that must be heard."

At the word "free" the crowd suddenly grew. Every person who had come to the markets was now ready to hear what the once famed Freydis Spits had to say.

"I see death!" Freydis yelled with a tremble on her lips. "Death in the Northern Sea."

From where she stood at the back of the crowd, Mathilde Nordstrom let out a sharp cry. Surely Freydis didn't mean Haroyld.

Around Mathilde, the rest of the crowd gasped and reeled back with horror. While Freydis' prediction about an early winter hadn't come true, her prediction about a Great Winter had. Now, their trust in the fortune teller had risen. Freydis' belief in herself was also inflating. The prediction about the captain's son had been a blip – a slight blemish – a mere mistake. But now, piece by piece, shell by shell, her predictions were coming true once more. And this one was a killer.

"Everyone – dead!" Freydis yelled even louder than before. Her voice wailed through the village and echoed up into the hills. It made mice flee from their burrows, bears tremble in their winter caves and owls take flight into the charcoal sky. "Everyone on board the *Plucky Leopard* will drown and the ship will sink to the bottom of the sea. That's right," Freydis said to a boy whimpering beside her leg. His father was a member of the crew. "There will be nothing left to make the ship into something new. There'll be no Sunken Leopard. No Dead Leopard. No Sinking Seal. The ship will go down and not a plank of its wood, or a member of its crew, will ever be found."

"WHALE!"

"The air is changing," Oona said to Barnacles the cat. "We must be getting very far north now." Though her map lay open before her, Oona had no idea where upon it they currently were. Haroyld had taught her how to use the stars for direction, but he had not shown her how to calculate distance. "It smells different." Oona sniffed the night air. "Like there are no smells left any more."

Barnacles raised his head towards the sky and twitched his whiskers. Then, he twitched his nose. He meowed at Oona – the loudest meow she had ever heard – and then he meowed again.

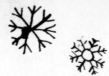

"What is it, Barnacles?" Oona said. He was trying to tell her something, but she had no idea what.

Barnacles left Oona's side and paced up and down the deck. A few times he jumped on to the rail and pawed at the sky. Eventually, after doing this same thing six times, he returned to Oona and let out a long, mournful cry.

"I know," Oona said. She leant down and tried to pat Barnacles, but the cat jumped away. He liked her a lot more now, but he still wouldn't let her touch him. "I miss Haroyld too. I hope he wakes up soon."

For two days the men of the *Plucky Leopard* hunted for a whale without success. Then, on the third day, a spout of water shot out of the sea.

"There she blows!" a man cried from the ship's tallest mast. He had seen a splash of white as the water crashed back into the ocean. "Whale!" he screamed. "Whale on the starboard side!"

Within seconds of the sighting, the captain changed course. The *Plucky Leopard* turned east. The wind was on their side, and the ship ploughed gamely after the beast.

The whale fled from the ship full of cold and

tired men. With lanterns tied to the bow, the ship kept chase. The flames flickered across the water below, lighting the way ahead.

As the *Plucky Leopard* drew close, the men prepared the whaleboats.

"Not long now, boys!" the captain cried joyfully into the night. "Looks like we'll be taking a whale home after all."

While the captain yelled at his men, Barnacles grabbed the golden steering wheel and turned it sharply to the right. A second later, the captain's boot kicked him in the back and sent him sprawling across the deck.

"Be off with you, stupid cat!" the captain yelled. His eyes flared with rage. "No one touches my wheel."

Barnacles got back on his paws and pounced at the wheel for a second time. The captain grabbed him by the scruff of the neck and threw him to the ground. Just before the captain gave him a kick strong enough to send him right over the rail, Barnacles scampered away.

Stowaways, rotten fish and cold water! Barnacles cursed to himself. He could play a fiddle, read a crew list and scale the tallest mast on his ship in under five seconds, but he could not speak a word of human. This had hardly troubled him before. But now this skill was important. This was an emergency. There was an iceberg up ahead: he and the girl had smelled it. And now his ship, his ninth and final ship, was heading straight towards it.

As soon as the whale was sighted, the captain ordered Oona below deck. He did not want her to ruin another hunt. Instead of going to the storeroom, Oona went to the navigator's cabin. She sat down beside Haroyld and rolled out his new map.

"I've almost finished," Oona said to Haroyld. Two weeks had passed since he dived into the sea and he had yet to stir. But his skin was no longer blue and he was breathing freely. Oona thought he would wake soon and then he could guide them home. "I've marked all the places that you marked on mine, and I've even drawn a tavern to mark Nordlor."

Oona was putting more ink on the map when a shudder ripped through the ship. To Oona, it felt like the heart of the *Plucky Leopard* was being torn out and hurled into the sea. She jumped off the floor and ran over to the porthole.

Oona looked outside. Instead of seeing the ocean, she saw a wall of ice.

"ABANDON SHIP!"

When Oona reached the deck, chunks of ice rained down around her. As she had raced up the stairs, a man had raced below to check on the damage. He returned with bad news.

"There are holes," he said to the captain. "At least ten. All through the hull. Each one is bigger than the breadth of a man."

The captain ordered his men to make a line that led from the ship's hull to the deck. Then, using buckets, they scooped the icy water out. But no matter how quickly they worked, more water flooded in.

The *Plucky Leopard* sank lower into the sea.

The captain watched the water rise and realized what they had to do.

"Abandon ship!" he screamed. "Take to the whaleboats!" he cried across the night. And then, like the northern saying went, he raced towards the nearest whaleboat and was the first to abandon his ship.

While the men of the *Plucky Leopard* raced to abandon ship, Oona raced back below deck.

"Haroyld," Oona said. "Haroyld, you have to wake up."

Oona pulled on the navigator's arm, but he did not move.

"Please, Haroyld," she begged as tears rolled down her face. "I'm too small to carry you."

By now the water had escaped the ship's hull and was swirling around Oona's feet. It felt like she was standing on the sea cobbles back home, only this water was rising and there was no stone to hold it back.

The water had risen to Oona's knees when the door to the navigator's cabin swung open. Oona wondered which of the men had come down to help. When she turned around she realized that none of them had.

"Barnacles?" Oona said. "What are you doing here?"

To avoid the rising water, the cat pounced on to the navigator's trunk and then on to his bed. He was carrying his fiddle. At first Oona thought he was going to play a song as the ship went down, but instead of plucking the strings he raised the instrument above his shoulders and slammed it on to the navigator's head.

The wood shattered and splintered. Barnacles' prized fiddle snapped in two. Then, the navigator moaned and opened his eyes.

"Oona," he said. "You're alive." He smiled weakly and slowly sat himself up in bed. Then, he noticed the water.

"Hurry, Haroyld." Oona tugged on the navigator's arm. "We have to get out of here. The ship is sinking."

The water had risen to Oona's waist, and the navigator's belongings floated on top.

Oona helped Haroyld out of bed. Barnacles, not wanting to get wet, jumped on to the navigator's shoulder. Then, they pushed their way over to the door and waded towards the stairs. When they stepped out on to the deck, they looked towards the spot where the whaleboats were kept.

Oona's heart sank. All four of the whaleboats were gone. In their panic to escape the sinking ship, the men of the *Plucky Leopard* had fled and left them there to drown.

THE FLYING LEOPARD

"Come back," Oona screamed into the night. "Come back and save us!" she bellowed across the sea. The boats were so close Oona could see the men huddled inside. But instead of turning and coming back towards them, the four whaleboats continued to drift away. Soon, they were just shadows and then memories in the night.

"Perhaps they did not hear us," Haroyld said softly. Though he and Oona knew their words had carried far.

The stars in the sky grew brighter as the ship sank lower into the sea. Water flooded out from below the deck and began to flood the deck itself. Though Haroyld knew the way home, the ship was too broken to take them there.

As the icy water closed in, the girl, the cat and the navigator huddled together. All was silent until the navigator spoke.

"Did you know," Haroyld said, "that I used to have a daughter?"

Oona shook her head.

"Her name was Nora. She died before she even got the chance to live. But if she had lived, I would have liked her to be just like you."

"Like me?" Oona said. "But why?"

"Because you're brave, Oona: brave enough to stand up to your father and sneak aboard this ship. And you're kind: kind enough to dive into the sea and save a man who would not risk his own life to save you. And you've got the North in your blood. Why, I think you're splendid, Oona. Splendid in every way. And I couldn't be prouder, not even if you were my own daughter."

Despite the danger they were in, the navigator smiled and Oona smiled back. They only stopped when water lapped at their knees.

"Make for the mast, young Oona," Haroyld said. "It's higher up there."

Oona, Haroyld and Barnacles ran across the deck. When they reached the mast, Barnacles scampered up first. Then, Oona and Haroyld followed. As Oona helped the navigator into the crow's nest, she feared this was the end: she, Haroyld and Barnacles would drown and freeze in the deadly Northern Sea. But then something caught her eye. Above her head a trail of lights – of purples and greens and shimmering gold – made the inky heavens dance. The Northern Lights were back.

"It's a nardoo," Oona said.

As the girl, the cat and the navigator watched, a nardoo breached the water beside the ship. Its scales glistened grey and green and silver in the night. There was a scar on its back, right in the centre, where an old injury used to be.

"It's the one you saved," Haroyld said. "That's where you pulled out your father's harpoon."

As the three of them watched, the nardoo's scales changed. No longer hard and cold, they grew soft and fluffy. The scales turned to feathers, and the fins turned to wings. The nardoo lifted itself out of the water and swam into the sky.

A large jolt and a long shudder rocked the *Plucky Leopard*. The ship moved. But it didn't move forward or back, nor did it move to the right or to

the left. It didn't even move down into the dark, icy sea. Instead, the *Plucky Leopard* moved up.

As the ship rose into the sky, the water that had flooded into the *Plucky Leopard* now flooded back out. It crashed down on to the water below until only a few droplets remained. Then, they too trickled downwards and fell like rain on to the ocean.

The nardoo – the flying nardoo just like the one in her birthday story – pulled them up towards the Northern Lights. They passed through the rainbow clouds and into the sky beyond. The whole of the Northern Sea stretched out below them.

"Would you look at that?" Haroyld said. "Its just like one of my maps."

Oona looked down at the world and smiled. Beside her, Barnacles looked down as well. He didn't look amazed. He looked frightened. Before he could jump away, she scooped him into her arms and gave him a hug. "Don't worry," she assured the cat. "You're not going down with your ship. Not tonight. You're going up. We're all going up." She gave him another squeeze, and she swore she heard the grumpy cat purr.

The ship began to float through the sky. Haroyld looked down at the world below and then up at the stars.

"Why I never," he said softly.

"What?" Oona asked. "What is it?"

"We're flying south," he said. "The nardoo: it's taking us home."

Though it had taken three months for the *Plucky Leopard* to reach the spot where it hit the iceberg, it took the nardoo less than three hours to fly it home.

"There's Mournful Harbour," Haroyld said as the blue water beneath them gave way to white snow. The river that led south had frozen over and snow had settled upon its surface. "And that there is the town of Whitlock. And look, Oona. Look down there." Haroyld pointed towards the south where a speck of orange light shone amid a white world. "That's Nordlor. We're almost home."

"Three blasted months," Freydis muttered as she pulled the elk-skin cloak tighter around her body. That was her punishment for predicting the future: a three month ban from Nordlor for inciting panic and uproar. The elders had decided it. After all, her latest prediction hadn't only upset one person. It had upset the entire village. They thought it best for everyone to have a break from the fortune teller and her horrid predictions.

But they would invite her back, thought Freydis. It was only a matter of time. She couldn't wait for the day the sea robin flew into harbour with the news: news that the *Plucky Leopard* had sunk and everyone was dead.

"That will show them," Freydis said. She bet they would welcome her back with open arms. Well, maybe not open arms. But they would start paying for her futures again. And when she had enough money she would move on to another village or town. The great Freydis Spits would be famed once more.

But for now, Freydis had been ostracized from the village and her new home was a tent down by the river. She had stolen some sealskins to keep her warm, but they weren't doing a good job. She was about to fetch some sticks to make a fire when she heard the faint sound of laughter and two people crying out, "Hurrah! We're home!"

Freydis poked her head out of the tent and looked around.

"Who's there?" she hissed.

No one replied, yet the laughing and yelling continued. It took several more minutes for Freydis to realize the sounds weren't coming from around her but above. Slowly, she looked up towards the night sky. A ship flew overhead. And it wasn't just any ship either. In the moonlight, three golden words glimmered on its starboard side: *The Plucky Leopard*.

Freydis wailed and screamed like a wounded bear. "The blasted ship was meant to sink, not flaming fly!"

This was it. Her reputation was ruined. In tatters. Broken beyond repair! There was no coming back from this. So, before anyone in the village woke up, and despite the dangers of travelling by foot, she threw on her elk-skin cloak, grabbed her stick of shells and rattled off into the night. Forget finding the future in the North. Forget everything about the North. She was going to go south. Apparently, it was a lot nicer down there.

At two in the morning, like clockwork, the shutters of the Nordstroms' cottage blew open. When she tried to close them, Mathilde could not believe what she saw. Right there in the sky, floating above the frozen river, was the *Plucky Leopard*.

Forgetting all about the shutters, Mathilde left the cottage and raced down to the dock. She got there just as the *Plucky Leopard* landed with a thud and then a crack on the frozen river. For a moment it looked like the ship was going to sink, but the ice held strong and it balanced on top instead of slipping beneath.

Mathilde's eyes had been locked so intently on the ship that she did not notice the creature who carried it until it began to fly away.

Having rescued the girl who had rescued it, the nardoo let go of the ship and rose once more into the sky. It turned north and swam up through the stars. For the first time in history, the Northern Lights danced in the skies above Nordlor. With everyone else in Nordlor asleep, Mathilde was the only villager to see it.

Mathilde thought she would never see anything as magical as the nardoo again, but only one minute later she was proved wrong. Two figures emerged from a gaping hole in the hull. Even from a distance, Mathilde recognized them. It was Haroyld, her husband, and Oona, the captain's seventh daughter. The latter was holding Barnacles the cat. Mathilde let out a cry of delight and ran across the ice to greet them.

AN UNWANTED WEDDING GIFT

Two Months Later

"We've spotted something, Captain," a man said from the deck of the *Keeling Fox*. "Something in the water."

"A whale?" the captain asked hopefully. This was the longest hunt they had ever been on. Winter had almost passed, and they were still two hundred miles into the Icelands. It was a miracle they hadn't frozen to the sea.

The man shook his head. "It's a ship. No. Boats. Four of them, full of men."

"Well, drop one of ours. Go out and see who

they are."

The man gathered three others, and they rowed out into the icy sea. They bobbed beside the other boats for a few minutes before rowing swiftly back.

"They've gone crazy, Captain," the man said upon his return. "They're all mad."

"What do you mean, boy?"

"Well, they keep talking about flying ships and fish that swim through the sky. Should we leave 'em?"

The captain of the *Keeling Fox* thought for a moment and then shook his head. "Better not. Bring them on board."

The four boats were hauled on to the ship. The men inside scampered on to the deck and kissed the wood. One amongst them approached the captain. He started to ramble words that did not make sense.

"And then it flew," the man finally said. He wore the hat of a captain – a hat decorated with a golden leopard – but he did not look like a captain now. His clothes were in tatters, icicles hung from his beard and he had lost so much weight you could see the shape of his skeleton beneath his sallow skin. "And my knife!" the man cried. He grabbed at the captain's jacket and searched his pockets.

"Have you seen my knife? I think it fell into the sea." The man started to cry and beat his fists against the captain's chest.

"This one's the craziest of the lot," the man who fetched them said.

"Stark-raving mad," the captain agreed. "Better lock him below deck. Don't want him scaring the other men. We'll drop him off at Fisherman's Hell on the way home. They'll be able to look after him there."

Despite the absence of Trine, who had fled with the gardener Hermann two days before, the wedding of Prince Turnip to five of the Britt sisters ended up being a terribly grand affair. People came from all over the South to hear them say their vows. There were so many guests that the castle could not house them, and five hundred were forced to watch the ceremony from the turnip fields.

One hundred chefs were hired for the catering. They created all sorts of wondrous dishes: turnip truffles, turnip tarts and savoury turnip jelly. They even crafted a special turnip wine which held the juice of thirty turnips in each bottle.

"But you can't drink it yet, ladies," Prince Turnip warned his five new wives. "It must have time to age. Ten years should do it."

But while the Britt sisters may have had to wait for the turnip wine, they were now allowed to see what was housed in the northern wing.

"Come now, ladies. Hurry! Be quick," the prince cried as he led them out of the Great Hall. He had a skip in his step. "It's time to see the northern wing."

The Britt sisters and their mother followed the prince as he led them across the courtyard.

"I'm sure you're all going to love the northern wing," the prince said. "Now that we're married it will be your new home. Here we go."

The prince stopped outside a large stone door. He drew an iron key from his pocket and turned it in the lock. The lock clicked, and the door creaked open. Air as cold as the North crept out into the warm sunshine. For the first time since they entered the South, the Britt sisters shivered.

"Aren't there any fireplaces in this part of the castle?" Ina asked.

"No. No. No. Most certainly not," the prince said with a shake of his head. "That would ruin the effect."

"The effect of what?" Berit asked.

"The winter effect. When you live in the North winter lasts all year long."

"The North?" Sissel said. "But we're in the South. Aren't we?" Suddenly she looked confused and unsure, like maybe they hadn't caught a carriage over the border after all.

"Not when you're in the northern wing. Here, I'll show you."

Prince Turnip stepped inside. The captain's wife and her five daughters followed. As their eyes adjusted to the darkness (along with fireplaces, it appeared that no candles were allowed in the northern wing either) they gasped and reeled back with horror. Though none of them had ever entered the northern wing of Turnip Castle before, the room looked awfully familiar.

"Look," Prince Turnip cried with delight. "It's just like Nordlor only smaller. My grandfather had it built one hundred years ago. Isn't it wonderful? It cost him two thousand golden crowns to make it all."

"But it was meant to be full of treasure," Sissel cried.

"Treasure?" the prince said. "Why of course it's full of treasure." He pushed his five new wives in deeper. The further away from the door they moved the colder the room became. Soon their breath came out in clouds of white and their skin turned

249

very pale. Homes, just like the ones in Nordlor, branched out around them. In the distance, they could see the third floor of their own home: the one made from the broken wreckage of the *Limping Lynx*.

Beneath their feet, the cobbles moved as if waves were trapped beneath them. Even the air smelled like the air in real Nordlor: of salt and fish and whale oil smoke. The only difference was the sky. Instead of seeing a bright sun above their heads, grey stone and cobwebs adorned the dark ceiling.

"I've always loved the North," the prince continued. "Nordlor in particular. 'The Village of One Thousand Ships,' my grandfather called it. He was too afraid to travel all the way up there himself, so he built a replica all the way down here. He loved the North even more than me. Spent his whole life building this collection." Prince Turnip waved his hands around the room. "He collected maps and fish and barrels of whale oil. He even bought the broken mast of the *Wandering Walrus*. Apparently," the prince whispered, leaning towards his wives, "that was the greatest whaler that ever sailed."

The five Britt sisters whimpered. Then, so too did their mother. Somehow, they had found the only man in the South who loved the North more than their father.

"So," Prince Turnip continued, oblivious to their displeasure, "you can imagine my surprise and utmost joy when Gertrund told me there were seven Nordlor ladies stealing turnips in the northern fields. I said, 'Right, Gertrund. Take me to them now. I'm going to marry those young ladies and add them to my collection.'"

By now they had reached a replica of the Sinking Eel, and it made the Britts cry even louder.

"So that is what I am going to do," Prince Turnip said loudly, so he couldn't hear their cries. "Along with Little Nordlor I now have five Nordlor girls and an old Nordlor woman too! My grandfather would be so proud."

Before his five new wives and his mother-in-law could escape, Prince Turnip bade them farewell, raced outside and locked the door to the northern wing behind him.

OONA'S SHELL

Far off in the distant north, spring had come to the real town of Nordlor. The mountains had thawed. Snow melted away and green grass sprouted out. The animals in the hills – the bears, the foxes and the little mice – left their winter slumber and awoke to a new year.

Two months had passed since the *Plucky Leopard* landed on the frozen surface of Nordlor Harbour. The iceberg had broken the ship beyond repair, and now it stood in the black sand of Nordlor's shore. But it wasn't going to be turned into a tavern or a house. It was going to be made into a whole new ship. They would remove the broken planks of wood and rebuild it. The ship wouldn't be as large as the *Plucky Leopard*, but it would still hold the girl, the cat and the navigator.

"And when it's ready," Haroyld said to the girl sitting beside him, "we will sail to all the towns along the northern shore and make a new map of the North together. And we're going to make copies this time," he said. "Copies so it's never lost at sea again."

Oona smiled up at the navigator. Since returning to Nordlor, she had been living with Haroyld and Mathilde. For the first time in her life, she felt like she was with her real family: like on the night she was born she should have been born in a house hewn from the *Little Skipper*, not the *Sinking Eel*. This was where she belonged and who she belonged with.

An old cat pulled Oona from her thoughts. He rubbed against her leg and meowed with pleasure. In his two hundred years of life, Barnacles had never looked so proud or grand. Not only had he become the first sea cat to fly in the sky, he was also going to be the first sea cat in history to have ten ships instead of nine.

Oona, Haroyld and Barnacles were about to go to

lunch – Mathilde was making an asparagus spring tart – when something brushed against Oona's shoe. It was a shell. She picked it up and held it to her ear. Waves crashed inside. They sounded like the waves in the North. Then, they changed. Water turned to words, and the whisperings of a future trickled into her ear.

OONA BRITT WILL GO SOUTH AND EAST
AND WEST AND NORTH.
SHE WILL GO FURTHER THAN ANY MAN OR
WOMAN HAS BEEN BEFORE.
SHE WILL SAIL THE WORLD IN HER VERY OWN SHIP;
A SHIP CALLED THE *DAZZLING PEARL*.

"Haroyld," Oona said. She turned to the old man sitting beside her and smiled. "Forget making a map of the North. Let's make a map of the entire world!"

Don't miss

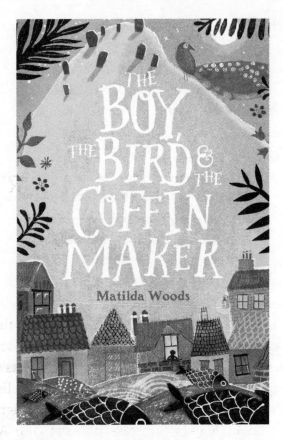

Alberto is a coffin maker, spending his quiet days creating the final resting places for people in the town of Allora. Then one day a mysterious boy named Tito and his magical bird arrive – flying from danger and searching for a safe haven. Can Alberto shelter them from the town's prying eyes and the shadows of their past?

This is a story of life and death and of how hope can burn bright in a place faded by sadness.

THE COFFIN MAKER'S
FIRST COFFIN

The town of Allora was famous for two things. The first was its flying fish and the second was the beauty of its winding streets. Tourists came from all over the country to watch the fish fly out of the sea while artists came to paint, in pigment, the bright houses that rose like steps up Allora Hill. There were so many colours that the artists did not have enough pigments to paint them, and it was rumoured (at least by the Finestra sisters) that the great artist, Giuseppe Vernice, invented a whole new colour just to paint the roof of their house.

"Splendid Yolk, it was called," Rosa Finestra said to anyone who would listen.

"Derived from the crushed eye of a peacock feather," Clara Finestra added with a wise nod.

Yet though the sisters gushed about their bright home, the one next door was even brighter.

Alberto Cavello's house was the highest house on the hill. If you went any higher you would reach the graveyard at the top. It stood like a bright azure jewel glistening across the sea. And it wasn't just bright. It was loud. It was loud when Alberto and his wife, Violetta, moved in. It grew louder when their first child, a girl named Anna Marie, was born; louder still when their son, Antonio, came into the world; and even louder when a little miracle named Aida wailed for the first time within its bright walls.

Alberto was a carpenter: the best in all of Allora. During the day he would build beds, tables and chairs for his paying clients, and at night he would build toys for his children.

With each new toy Alberto made, a new sound filled the house: squeals of delight as Anna Marie jumped off her spinning chair; screams of anger as Aida cried for Antonio to give back her favourite doll; and cries of "Gallop on! Gallop on!" as this same Antonio raced his wooden horse up and down the stairs.

Their house remained bright, loud and bustling for seven happy years until the sickness came.

The sickness appeared in the coldest month of winter, but it did not reach Allora until spring.

The first to fall ill were the men working on a new railway that linked Allora to the north, then the doctors who tended them and the artists who had come to paint the town. Only one family was wealthy enough to flee. The mayor took himself and his family on a long holiday to a place the sickness had not spread.

"Good luck!" he cried over his fat shoulder as a plush coach drawn by six white stallions carried them far away.

In the beginning, the dead were buried in the graveyard – one, then two, then three to a single plot – but as the sickness spread other measures had to be taken.

A gate was built at the back of the graveyard and a thin staircase carved into the stone with steps leading down to the water. No longer buried, the dead were wrapped in blankets and cast out into the violent, surging sea.

As the number of dead mounted and the number of living fell, the cobbled streets of Allora grew quiet. Houses went unpainted and shutters, once thrown open to greet spring, were pulled tightly closed. Even the Finestra sisters didn't poke their big noses out.

Just like the unfinished paintings that lay abandoned in the streets, the town of Allora itself began to fade.

The sickness rose up the hill – house by house – until it finally reached Alberto's home.

It took the eldest child first. Alberto spotted the purple mark behind Anna Marie's left ear as she read a book in her favourite chair. Then, Antonio fell ill. While he was ailing in his bed, the mark came upon little Aida.

Violetta and Alberto tended to each child as they fell sick. They kissed them when they cried, hugged them when they whimpered and when the time came for each of them to go they answered, "Yes, of course: one day, we will meet again."

Keeping her promise, Violetta joined them two days later. The plague bearers came to collect their bodies that evening, but Alberto wouldn't let them.

"I can't," he had said to the two men waiting at the front door. "I can't let you throw them away. Not into that cruel sea." Even from where he stood outside the highest house on Allora Hill, Alberto could see foam shooting up from where the waves crashed against the grey stones below. He could not bear to think of his family thrown in there.

"You must get rid of them somehow," the men had replied. "You can't let them stay inside. It will spread the sickness quicker."

"I'll bury them."

"All the coffin makers are dead. We collected the last one this morning."

"Then I'll make their coffins myself."

And that is what Alberto did. He went into his workshop and for the first time built something for the dead instead of the living. He carved a coffin for his wife, a coffin for his eldest daughter, a coffin for his only son, and a coffin for little Aida. Each was smaller than the one before and, like Babushka dolls, could fit inside the other.

When the coffins were finished and his family buried, Alberto returned to his workshop and began to make his own. But by the time he finished, the plague had left the town. The mayor returned from his holiday, the Finestra sisters reopened their shutters and people passed gaily up and down the streets of Allora once more.

But instead of joining them, Alberto sat beside his coffin every day, waiting for the purple mark to come back and claim him too.